GLENDA REED

A SAPPHIRE
OUT OF TIME

Two sisters being lost in time

A Sapphire out of Time
Copyright © 2022 by Glenda Reed

ISBN
978-1-958690-02-4 (Paperback)
978-1-958690-03-1 (eBook)

TABLE OF CONTENTS

CHAPTER 1

"A Sapphire Out Of Time"

Surprisingly we saw a sign saying "Looking for a treasure?"

I called out, "Well, I'm packed and ready," waiting for my sister Elaine to give the go ahead to call our taxi to the airport. "Give me a few minutes and I'll be there."

I had been so excited and ready for a few days now, just daydreaming about our trip, and all the wonderful shops that we had not visited yet, even though we have been so many times, London was not a few Antique areas, and some shops, it was a world of its own. In the twenty-five miles of London area, there were thousands of antique areas.

One area, we had been to many times before, but did not have time to see very much, mainly because we wanted to do so many and never really had enough time. This time we had plenty of time.

Or so we thought and we had planned time wise.

Antiquing was our thing, we both had things in our homes that would invite a thief if they ever caught a glimpse of some of the things we had found through the years. So now we are off again.

Ghosts were my interests. What we did include, were both her likes and mine. The plans were made and the tickets were bought, and another sister trip was in the works once again.

Finally we were off to make more dreams we had been traveling since we were kids. Mostly to Sarasota Florida to our Grandmothers beautiful home and the beach.

Hanging up the phone after buying our tickets, on this last call, we were both so excited for another dream vacation, and this was not our first trip by far.

Elaine and I both, had spent a lot of time, before we decided where to go, so when we made these reservations we made sure that when we arrived we did not want to go sleep, but go straight to antiquing, and that if we could sleep on the plane,

From the medicine my Doctor gave me, we could drop our bags, which were not heavy because we made our plans way in advance and wanted room for our next buys,if our purchases were too big we shipped them home and if they were small we carried them in our bags, in case we found something we could not live without,

London was a treasure trove of history, and we had seen many antiques rarely seen in other countries. And we had bought our share on other trips, but we were still on the hunt for two special antiques, the one she was pursuing, and the Grandfather clock I have dreamed about so often.

Sometimes I thought my dreams were so real I would wake up in a sweat, thinking I was stuck inside a big tall clock, and it was huge, and I couldn't get out. I would be pounding on the glass front, looking out and seeing things like crazy images running all around me but they never saw me in there. I would wake up at home, and find I had been holding my breath. But I was in my bed shaking and crying.

Through the years we had compared dreams as little girls. But at that time in our life we soon forget the dreams until they came again, and being so small it never occurred to us it was unusual, we would cry to our mother who would sooth us and we would go back to sleep and not remember it at all and as we got older we began to remember the dreams that were still there again.

Sleep, if you call a small seat in a little space on a huge plane, sleeping, made me laugh out loud. In hopes of heading straight to the Antique area,, both of us expressedthe hopes, and feelings of a great ten days. In one of the many most famous Antiquitie areas in old London. Our idea of haunting antiques were both different and the same in Idea only. As we rode the plane we had some special moments and sisterly conversations, about our hopes for a dream and our hopes for the week ahead. Our plan was a few days longer this time. More time for searching.

CHAPTER 2

After the early morning arrival, and gloomy London was still the same old gloomy London, so taking the train into town, and then checking in to our favoritehotel near Covent Gardens, we hurriedlyput our things in the room, sitting our suitcase in the room by our beds and the only thing Itook hurriedly sticking it in my pockets,, and immediately headed out, taking no time for a quick nap or rest or even getting a cup of tea, straight into the busy streets we went, to explore all of our options for the first day.

And we couldn't wait, it was a beautiful sunny sky so far, surprising us, as the norm for London is half and half, rainy days, and since there were many streets, and we had a list of things we wanted to accomplish asap we were ready for whatever the day brought, as it turns out, or so we thought.

Elaine and I both had the same thing in mind, Antiques!

We had inherited our love of Antiques from our daddy, and we each knew we were looking for something different and we would most likely end up alone, by the end of the day, meeting up for our dinner...

As our day progressed, we were rubbing shoulders, with all the other antique searching people, walking down the familiar streets, but somehow in all our excitement, without noticing we took a different turn to haunt some new streets. Elains said we better write down this address to get back tonight,right?"I shook my head a positive yes.

All at once I saw a sign that took my breath away.I nudged Elaine as we walked, my mouth moving in these words! "Look"and we were both surprised and shocked, but both looking at the same thing,both of us were smiling,Antiques you only dream of finding, and then, I got my breath back, saying to Elaine"Oh my Gosh,read this one! "who was also so distracted in our new space.

To our amazement, these were new words and they silently were beckoning to both our hearts.

It simply said, and of course these were exactly the right words, that could draw everyone and anyone who was Antiquing that day inside this shop..

"A Sapphire out of time"

I spoke up first, saying, "Of course, look Elaine", her excitement was apparent, "somehow I think we were meant to be here today". Looking at her to see what she might be thinking, I saw her face lit up with excitement, "and I am eternally happy", I replied, then thinking about the word eternally, I wondered where that came from. I do not usually say eternally in any type of sentence or conversation. I felt like it came from somewhere else, but even Elaine was watching me, so I began another conversation and forgot what I had said. So, thinking hard, finally I was ready to move on,

I said "I can't wait to see what we find in the dark and gloom of this shop. Off to the left there was an old and gloomy-looking area bad enough to put someone off if they were so inclined to be frightened.

Pointing at the dark and gloomy store front, and, it must have been an omen, because of my birthstone, I said "remember my birthstone is a Sapphire…Blue..?"

Smiling, she shook her head yes. And she says, "if we see a door that says Garnets for sale I'm thinking it's an omen for both of us and today might be our day."

We were laughing, as we saw lots of people out so early in the morning. Probably because the weather was perfect today. Trying to walk side by side chatting was not so easy this morning. After a few bumps and going around this slow person, to find three more blocking out paths, we took an aggressive offence and stepped out into the edge of the street and making more strides we moved past the crowds as they wandered off to another street here and there.

Elaine's birthstone was Garnet, so we were laughing, and she said that today, if we ran into another sign that says Garnet out of time, the coincidence would be hard not to believe!

And that we also might be entering a time zone. Laughing out loud I nodded and said maybe.

A garnet out of time, well that would only be fair. If I found the Sapphire Antiques maybe somewhere here there was another Antique Store waiting for Elaine too. At the time it wasn't important and we kept walking and going in and out one Gallerie into another.

How could I have ever known what was about to happen? And if I had had a clue, what would I have done?

Well I did not know anything but the facts about our plan for today, justexcited to be together again,doing what we have both always loved, so there was something special in each step,we both kept walking around people, through the crowds on to our next adventure, eyes going everywhere, back and forth.I knew she was going to get worried, if we didn't see some kind of sign, somewhere for her,because somewhere in all these newer Antique shops we hoped there had to be a Suit of Armor with some sort of red color on the armor,on it just for Elaine, maybe red stones, embedded somewhere, we had no idea yet.

Even something red around the face of the armour, maybe this was what I had pictured when we talked at home years ago about when I talked to her about that dream.

It was what made it fun in the beginning, that we both had been searching for two items in our mind and that they were proving so hard to find.

And after we had searched and passed maybe the first 100 Antique stores along the way, going down alleys and back streets, and a few new countries,we were both still out there searching. The best part of traveling the world over was that we both owned our own businesses and did not have jobs that would hold us back, so we could take off whenever the urge hit us, because our lives had been good to us.

We both immediately turned toward this beautiful Blue door that had attracted our attention. When my hand first touched this door knob, I immediately felt a shocking stinging in my hand so strong that I jerked my hand off, as I was walking up into this old beautiful door of a very very oldAntique Shop,it had actually shocked my fingers and I felt a jolt running through my body, and it was so painful that looking down to see if there was a carpet of fabric that could have caused the static electricity that had stung my fingers, I saw there was none.

I instantly wondered how that beautiful door, in this old area of south London, could appear so beautiful, and new, and old, and ancient, at the same time. Holding my hand to my chest Elaine said "are you alright"and I shook my head yes.

CHAPTER 3

Moving on, I mentioned the shock of touching the Bizarre old Blue Door, and I noticed she pushed it open behind me and felt nothing."ok"I said to myself.

Both of us mentioned that this was the first time we had ever seen anything that looked new in this part of the older shopping district, full, with Antiques written all over it. Within a moment we were on to something else, forgetting the Blue Door totally.

As we went on we talked again about what I had felt. But we were too excited and virtually charged with a new energy to think about this shock that had passed through my body right then. So we just wentinto different doors and forgot about the blue door for the time being.

So for us being back again, hunting Antiques, in London's most famous Antique District was a thrill of its own. When I think of how many times in the past ten years I have flown to London to haunt these shops, and as always the next time was as thrilling as the first one.

The Blue Door should have sent a message to my brain, something like "hey what the heck was the shocking feeling about".

Always planning for the next trip gave us both an exciting outlook for our future, this year or next year I remember once I said to my sister that maybe we were time travelers, meaning that the Antiques had pulled us from Pillar to Post in the last ten years of our travels. Remembering all the fun times one after another.

I remember many times lately, thinking how lucky we were to both be interested in Antiques. As in some families each sister or brother had their own likes, we were so lucky, to enjoy each other so much and to have similar interests, which we both had gotten from our Daddy. When we were very young every Friday night at the top of Frankfort Street there was an antique auction. Daddy took us with him at different times. Both my sister and I learned a lot about the Antiques in our little corner of Woodford County, at those times.

Both of us began loving antiques at an early age.

We were a very close family, and one parent or the other always had us with them, like Fridays Mother got her hair done like clock work, and on Thursdays, my Father had his weekly insurance meetings, and he would take our mother and both of us with him to Lexington, and the girls shopped, while he worked.

I was always looking and searching for the right purchase, and I had had it pictured in detail in my mind for ages, a tall huge ancient Grandfather Clock. And there was no reason for this except I had dreams about a huge Grandfather Clock, which turned into nightmares as time moved on.

CHAPTER 4

Once a long time ago, I had dreamed about it since I was a child. I remembered waking up and screaming, until my Mother came running in and asked me to sit up, saying ``what were you dreaming about dear, that has upset you so much?''"I told her I was locked into a great big clock and couldn't get out and you came and opened the door for me,"and then she would hand me a glass of water, that always seemed to be sitting right there to take my mind off the dream, and not wake up my little sister.When we were young we shared the same room and the same big bed. Many good times were had there. And then we grew up and got our own rooms.

She went off to college and I got married at sixteen.

We were always a close family, with perfect parents. The kind you read about but never give that another thought.

So today, since I have always felt there was a small street in this area, that had been calling out to me, even though I did no know it existed at the time, I was happy and yes I had always loved this area, but we noticed, there was no way anyone could distinguish which Antique Shop to go into first, because you wanted to see all of them on this street, and this onewas the one, I already knew itwas going to be one of my personal favorite streets.

I felt like a pro and I could just look and often enough I could feel if it was right or not.

But still never finding what we were looking for made me feel inferior.

I was here again, but today as we walked slowly down a side street, I suddenly was struck by a strange but happy feeling it was moving in on me. We were going to have lady luck on our side. I don't know why I said that then, but I was giddy with unexpected happiness and I honestly didn't know why.

Actually I wasn't even thinking that way.

Elaine said what's that look on your face? Have you researched this street or something? Do you know something I don't know"?

Asking Elaine if she was as excited as I was, she shook her head yes, and I never answered her because I was so excited. At that time I did not know why or what but I had a feeling something big was coming.

Together we both had high expectations for this trip, because this was a new area for both of us. I said "remember the Bobsy twins", and Elaine smiled and shook her head,

"Well we are the Antiquing searching sisters' ' laughing we moved on...simply forgetting the Blue Door and the shocking feeling I had experienced.

For some strange reason, at first I thought there was something very familiar in this area, looking around at everything as I walked down the street, and in a door to one of these Antique Shops, I took a step backward as if someone had shoved me suddenly and hard.

And then like I heard someone say out loud but only I could hear it, "Hello again", this time louder, so I looked at Elaine to see if she had heard it too, and yet she acted normal, looking in every window we passed, and so nothing came to mind, but a overwhelming happy feeling that at times just overwhelmed me. What the feeling was, at that point, I just could not tell, and I knew I had no idea where I was heading..

It seemed like I had forever been on the lookout for a certain GrandFather Clock. I had always hadthe picture of it somewhere in mind, after the dream when I was a child, but I had forgotten about it for years and then in History Class with Miss Hanson, my teacher, who was so old, and so into history that when one Thursday afternoon we opened up our book to begin to study England, in King Henry the eighth Reign, a lot of the things we talked about made me want to say "Oh no that isn't right,"but then I made myself keep quiet. I was shocked at myself, who was normally not talkative in class and usually never had answers on the spur of the moment. I sure did not want the kids to think I was showing off, and I really felt like an oddball in the room that day. I simp;y knew too much,and it was not written like I remembered it. But then how did I remember anything like that? That was not me? Now I think "or was it"

Page after page I had feelings that I already knew, about this and then something else would register in my mind about the old Castles or something this King was doing, and the furniture description was all wrong, all of a sudden I held my hand up, then I dropped it quickly, hoping none of my stuck up smart classmates saw me. And I felt like I knew what was going to be on the next page, I remember rubbing my head and my forehead until Dorothy, who was my best and closest friend said ``are you ok?"before we even were told to go to the next page or chapter. As we were reading the pages of information being the reason for the Magna Carta chapters, all at once Miss Hanson asked us a question about the legitimacy of this Queen and I spoke up without even holding my hand up to say "I know"it just came out of nowhere "that she was not the Royal Queen as the "King had not put the other one to death yet"there was a strange look in Miss Hansons eyes, so I acted like I was coughing and she let me have the hall pass to the bathroom.

I didn't want to shake my head but I did not know why I even spoke up at all. I was not an A student and never had been a history buff, until I opened my mouth that day. I think that dayit set something into motion for my future.

But back then all I was thinking was "what did I just open my mouth and say, because I have no idea why I, the shy, unpopular girl opened her mouth to say even a yes or no. That was not me. The smart sister was Elaine..

Miss Hanson was still looking at me and, I guessit was then that I knew what I had said was not anything I really even knew about. She began to question me, and as weird as it seemed, for a C student, I almost knew those answers, as if I had already studied the History book which I had not done, I was not the student who studied too much, just enough to make my Mother and Daddy happy.

Even when I was thirteen I did not put too much effort into my school work. I was loving the boys and my Dorothy.

So at that time she point blank asked me to enlighten her as to these "terrible turbulent times". When she said the word turbulent I once again started to hold up my hand, but then put it down because she was already on my case about my earlier remark. I remember looking down in my lap and trying to think why I said anything at all, but I did not know why.

With a look on her face that I did not get at all, It was, like I said, I was not the smart kid and I didn't even do my homework on time. Which I of course I could do, but was not the homework girl who did her homework on time very often. Oh yeah I got it done but not timely. There were times that I remembered things that we were reading, with a flash in my mind, but then I just thought I had heard her when teaching us this or that. So when she asked me what books I had been reading, I simply had no honest answer for her. I had not read anything yet.

But in my mind, there were pictures that would come and go, I would remember things and knowing full well I had nothing to base the memories or whatever they were on. When we were studying that era in history, and now I know for a fact that Miss Hanson was sooo smart, that I could not hide my thoughts or words that came out at the most inopportune time.

CHAPTER 5

The rest of my eighth-grade year, I was so careful because I saw her, she was always watching me, and calling on me to answer this or that and sometimes, as strange as it seemed, I could tell the answer, but how and why I have no ideas.. She would comment on things and then look at me, like she was waiting for an expression or answer, when I did answer her quickly she began to quiz me. And it was only me I noticed...Of course, I forgot this when the bell rang and we moved to the next room for a class that I was passing with a c- LOL.

She sat down beside me in the cafeteria one day and though I was sort of surprised, I did not show it to her at all. I had always disliked her because her way of teaching seemed to me that she wanted us to teach it and then to always have the right answers for her, but we were the learning students, I always thought I would make a better teacher than this old woman who was fixated on me. So after that day when I had answered her question, she had begun to ask me all sorts of things.

And shockingly I would speak out the answer. How I did that I had no idea. I could see her eyes fly open and I knew that what I had said, I really knew nothing at all about it. But I began to read the History homework, so she would not ask me anything I had not already read, and I even noticed that I felt like I had already known what was going to happen before I got to the answers. At twelve years old, I was only a dull, shy, average student. And with Elaine and her straight A's I really felt like a dummy. Our parents never gave me a hard time about school as long as I kept C's on the report card. So obviously I never put much effort out for school work, just enough to get by.

World History was the class I had picked out and had really enjoyed, until the day she asked and I answered without knowing how I knew that.

After that year I soon forgot how smart she had said I was, until I told her something that was not in this book and explained the way this really happened.

The subject was ladies ' clothing, and one girl in my class said that the women all hato wear bustles and wanted to know why. I jumped in and said "no those were not bustles, but bunched up undergarments to protect them when sitting in wooden chairs that were so uncomfortable."I saw Miss Hanson staring at me, and immediately sat down and kept quiet for the next thirty minutes, but I saw her looking at me and I knew she wanted more answers, when the bell rang I jumped up in front of Dorothy and ran out of the room.

Later I remember I was in the lunchroom, and I had a feeling someone was watching me, when I finally decided to check out the room, I Miss Hanson was looking at me and I was thinking "oh Lord don't her come over here again, because I really didn't like being the topic of discussion, and felt like she thought I was crazy, or maybe too smart, but that wasn't me, because I knew I was not too smart at all.And she always wanted to know how I knew this or that and I would say that I got it from the lesson and that maybe it was the way I wanted it to be"I would actually say anything to keep her from asking more questions those days. Knowing I probably had not even read the homework she gave us.

About that time I noticed there were things about the time period that enchanted me enough to want to read the lesson, and I did start reading the homework, and I remembered it was very interesting to me, and it felt sad to me sometimes, and that was an odd feeling for me who did not care a fig about history,.but I couldn't say why yet.

There was a boy Jackie McCray who was the SMARTEST, in the whole senior class, so I would let him take over whenever I could not get a word in. That really helped me because he knew all the answers and had studied, where I had not studied at all.

When I would go home Elaine and I would talk about Miss Hanson, and we would both laugh. Never once did any of this stay in my mind then.

When I look back on that time now I feel like there was something there I needed to learn but did not even try.

As we grew older we watched our Father who liked antiques and we both were his buddies, and little girls, so he would take us antiquing some days while my mother was getting her hair done. We loved it. It felt like fun and the thing about it was we both learned things that we never forgot.

There was a weekly auction in our little town and he loved to attend and sometimes we got to go with Daddy.

Through the years we grew up, Elaine and I went different ways. I married young, and she was in College. But Antiquing was in our blood. We did not know it then, but it was another bond we shared.

One day I was cleaning out a beautiful solid cherry wardrobe of my Great Grandmothers, her name was Mamma Todd, and I had always felt the love pouring over me when I had polished it for grandma, thinking about it being so old, and it had belonged to Grandma's mother,as a child, I had no idea really about these antiques then, but I was to learn.. It had been in the corner of her bedroom and my uncle had bought it for her when he was young and the story went that he had only paid $4 for it.

I mentioned it to my Daddy. He told me the wardrobe had a secret drawer inside another drawer, and when I found it, it was full of recipes my Grandmother had been keeping. They were very old and we thought they might have been her Mothers maby. When I took it to Elaine she said the same thing. It was not written in my Grandmother's writing which was very tiny and beautiful. So I often would look at it and wonder, who really took the time and wrote this, to myself.

But I still remember that was when we first talked to each other about antiques. My sister loved it as much as I was learning to. Many Saturdays Daddy would take us to the town's auction and we would watch him buy a piece of old furniture. Then when our Daddy died we took the antiques and divided them up between us girls. This was the start of our Antiquing. My traveling around the world with my husband also brought a new dimension to the word Antiques…

Amazingly to us both, we had grown fond of searching antiques out, and with my first trip to Scotland I found thousands of these shops. And when I was in England it was amazing the different Antique streets you could search. The third time I took my sister with me and together we hunted these Streets. Elaine had always wanted a certain Suit Of

Armor, explaining to me that she had seen it in a dream, the same story as I had had, the Grandfather Clock. Although my dream had started this epic Antiquing, I think it must have carried over to my sister. She had long since bought a huge Home and loved filling it up with beautiful small things then growing to larger pieces of furniture. So I began to entice her to travel with me, showing her my gifts I bought for myself, to (as I called it) Antique Heaven.

After about three trips together we were hooked!

And this time I brought my Sister Elaine with me, to haunt these new streets I had heard about, and all of them this time, together because she also had a certain item she wanted for her huge old home back in the Kentucky hills, up a holler on top of the mountain, and as far away as she could get from people. She had built a huge home there with 25 rooms. I always loved to visit and her cats would be in my bed before I fell asleep every time, one night I woke up and a cat was licking my hair.

For years she had been longing for a Suit of Armor. Together we had many conversations about why and where or even questions like, would we ever stumble upon these odd items we wanted. And for a long time and there were many times, when we were together, we had even pictured it in our minds. But we had never found one that would suit her expectations yet...

Moving forward in time!

CHAPTER 6

We were moving slowly down a side street, with arm to arm people, and here and there were new shops. There was one, when I came to it that was pulling at my heart, I felt it, I looked at her to see if she felt anything, but obviously she didn't yet. I said to my sister come on let's go inthis one feels like it wants to meet us and our American Dollars, laughing we walked in, it was dark, I had the feeling that I was being led forward by a soft sense just touching my right shoulder, then there was a flight of stairs and we walked up them, just like we knew where we going. And, we certainly did not know where we were going This was a very odd feeling but we kept glancing at each other and walking or climbing.

After walking up to a different kind of shop in front of a huge door we looked up, and the huge door started to open, like it was automated, but it was not, then creaking with all the effort of probably being shut for many years, I suspected. At first I was surprised at the dim lighting here, and I thought it was too dark...How would we find anything in this darkness?

Looking around I saw Elaine pointing to the torches on the walls, they were the only major source of light. I hadn't noticed yet, when Elaine spoke up, "What in the world is this about? Torches"? Elaine asked to no one in particular.

Not seeing lighting anywhere else. Shivering from a chill, I had a laughing idea, so I said maybe there was a ghost following us around, and he was laughing at us. I asked, Elaine, do you feel like we are alone here?" she laughed, "well sister there is no such thing as ghosts that I know of, but normally I would say "if you say so,"it feels like someone or something is either watching us or is here with us right now."that in itself was an odd remark from her, the non-believer of ghosts. I don't believe in them either but it was certainly an odd feeling I had while we walked.

We both laughed, and Looking back and forth, seeing nothing, we both just went forward. I loved my sister, and antiquing with my sister just felt right. We both had the Antiquing urge. Speaking up Elaine said exactly what I was thinking.

"Well I can't believe it, this is a first, I have never seen so many antiques in one place.

I mentioned motioning with my hands, to Elaine, "I have a feeling this time we are heading towards something important. Trust me we certainly have visited many of the antiques shops in London before, and most of them together but I don't remember this street."

"I told you I had a surprise for you and us."she said. Lol "I could not wait to see it, from this article."

She pulled it from her purse to show me."Here it is".

"What I saw was an article in a London newspaper one Sunday morning and cut it out so I could research the address, so hopefully we could find it the next time we crossed over the pond."

We both loved calling the Ocean the pond, as a joke our trips into the past took over our lives and when our parents both passed on, we both quit our Jobs to open an Antique shop in Boston like the ones we loved in England.

Elaine had brought the small article she read in the Sunday Newspaper one month ago, with her to surprise me.

It was times like these that I knew how much we had in common even if earlier, as younger siblings we had no idea, but these trips had pulled us together. And this bond felt just right. And I knew without a doubt Mamma and Daddy were smiling at us from heaven.

And the article mentions this shop, the fine writing from another visitor written underneath the article only said "maybe hard to see because I was in there and you couldn't see your hand in front of you, but I remembered the name of the store. A very Unusual name."

"The Creepy Century Clock Antiques"

"This street was not even on my secret list of "Antiques of one not to miss ``, she told me. Holding the article out for me to explore.

I said to Elaine "by far this is going to be the most fun of all. And to think it's all new to us.. She said "yes I know and how was it, we have never seen this one before sister, because you know we search and find each and every old moldy Shop!

"We never minded going back to the shops we had bought from before because things were bought and sold and acquired on a daily basis in these streets in London. Actually we had read people came from all over the world to hunt these streets. So of course that included my sister and I.

We finally found the shop listed in her little article. So we both looked all around so we would remember which way we were going when we came out. And it was really dark when we usually left.

The streets all looked so much alike and everyone of them grabbed your attention because this was the District by far the oldest in London and this particular area we had not been into before. We talked about this, the fronts and the only thing that made them different was the item they had in their front windows.

Walking into the dimly lit first room, we were stunned. Looking left and right having no idea which way we wanted to go, we both said almost in unison,"Wow, look at this inventory, this is more than I have seen in a long time, in most shops, and I go almost every weekend even at home, even when you have other plans I go hunting for my dream Grandfather Clock,"Elaine laughed at my seriousness to find my dream clock".

CHAPTER 7

When my sister and I go Antiquing we do double duty using my list and then we do her list. So my secret list was used up. Now, it was her list we had started on today happily.

Elaine said, "Remember about two months ago when I went to the Antique Festival in Charlotte? Well I picked up some paperwork there, and I saw these Antique Shops were advertising. So I tore it out and kept it in my wallet."I was so happy she had found some new shops that I said "good work Sister".

I always keep some in my purse when I travel here. Talking as we walked through the musty, old, smelly shops I asked, "Elaine,"I asked, "why do you think I am looking for a special clock, and I feel like I'm being forced to search out new antiques each year, and even though I have had good luck with lists, probably because I'm so intrigued and always searching for the Grandfather Clock of my dream, it never ends, and I'm off to another flea market or Antique Shop again and again."

"Do you know that feeling"? I waited for her answer.

"When I walk down these old side streets I feel like someone or something is calling my name, it almost sounds like It drives me or is begging meto hunt them out all the time and any place I can go. Do you know what I mean?"

"Yes sister, but don"t forget I'm on the hunt, also for mySuit Of Armor to stand in my foyer.

You know I have dreamed about it over and over again, and some nights Jim will shake me and laughingly say ``ELAINE, woohoo woohoo, come back now, your dream is beginning to haunt me and keeping me awake, and I do not need any Antiques that I know of."

Both of us laughed and said, I think we have seen maybe hundreds of Grandfather Clocks, and everytime you say "nope not this one, but we don't often see any suits of Armor do we?"her smile was wicked. And her eyes were big with excitement. Cold chills raced all over my body when she said those words.

Elaine started to tell me about a friend of hers who also travels and does antiquing. This particular one of her friends had visited Istanbul, and in the Bazaar she had seen a couple of Suits Of Armor. Which had set Elaine off on another adventure.

"We will be going to Istanbul next." Her statement was an order, as if already in the planning stages. But I loved traveling with her, so I'm ready for anything, and anytime. Together we had so much fun and every time we took a new turn or twist in the Antiquing markets was such a thrill to both of us. And she already knew that...

Smiling a big smile, she said "Next time you go to Scotland to see Eileen and her family I'm going to join you, but I'm telling you now we have to go to Istanbul first. I have a gut feeling my suit of armor is there waiting for me. Sometimes In the night and in my dreams I feel like I hear something calling me."

I saw the gleam in her eyes. And the hunt would be on. As soon as we could make it happen...

Recalling the trip where we had actually found a Grandfather Clock but not the perfect one 'Doesn't it seem funny that the one time we found my dream buy' that it was not for sale.""Yes I was almost in tears then all of a sudden I felt in my mind someone or something said "just let it go"So I did.

It felt like it was mine. It could not have been the one I'm searching for because if it were it would have spoken to me."I saw the look in her brown eyes, and I knew we both would eventually find our dream antique. I'm almost certain that I'm in touch with the Clock somewhere in the world, because I dream I hear ticking and more ticking then a voice says I'm here, and I'm waiting. I come awake instantly knowing it is my clock, but where it is I don't know. I didn't know when or how or where, but yes it was in the works as we both knew.

"We had found several Knights suits of Armor and just when we found THE ONE, it had a sign on it, "Not For Sale"do you remember when I touched it and I fell backwards? Something knocked me down, but there was not a thing there.

"Yes Elaine I do remember, we were so happy and shocked at the same time. Feeling like we were dreaming maybe, but no it was there, then you touched the big metal shoulder and said' "nope it is not the right one. You actually had a slight red mark on your hand, where you touched it. "Looking off into the darkness I just knew these memories would be our greatest treasure in days to come. Little did I know they were going to become nightmares!

CHAPTER 8

Traveling together, walking and talking to my sister was so much fun, the day was a bright sunny day, and in London you did not get many days like today, and we were taking advantage of every minute of sunshine, knowing rain was always in the forecast here...

Like last year, rain & more rain, umbrellas in your face or in your hair from passing so close to other people in the rain. Rubbers on our feet splashing through the puddles as we shopped, ducking in and out of doorways for shelter, rain or shine was our motto nowadays.

London arts and antique markets which were always my first stop on my way to Scotland and Eileen's house. She had traveled with me to go antiquing and then I would fly to Ayr and stay there for two weeks or longer sometimes,. and we would fly back home with our treasures.

My agenda was Scotland, where almost every year I visited Eileen, who was one of my dear friends. We were given each other's addresses at our Girl Scout Meeting, as eight-year-olds, in Scotland and I in Kentucky All of the girls were our age and while we were girl scouts and we were only eight years old, it seemed fun at first, but after some years we had no interest in our pen pals anymore. Thankfully Momma made me send the Christmas card and Birthday card, that was her way of keeping me in touch with her whether I liked it or not, I was soon to learn, Mamma was always right."Elaine, did you have a pen Pal?"I asked her, but I did notremember. If she had one also or not, I didn't remember...

"I don't remember if I had one or not."She said, and placing her finger by her nose I saw her eyebrows rise with her words "come on let's go."

Going to visit Eileen the first time, when I was 28 was the happiest time of my life. After that first trip I brought my husband or sister to Scotland, And to visit the antique shop with me. My husband did not care about Antiques, or the weather in Scotland.so when I mentioned a trip he always bowed out. Saying he knew how much I loved it but he had already been there with me twelve years in a row, so I finally asked my sister to come with me and after the first time she and I were ready to fly out at a moment's notice. Trying England we found the same abysmal weather. Soon it was just the two of us sisters.

Together, Eileen introduced me to Indian Curry's and with antique shopping, we went off the path and the little streets were so alike that after three hours my mind boggled down with the search for the just right perfect old Grandfather Clock. Soon the little streets all began to look alike.

Now when I visit I always make plans. The far North of Scotland turned out to be my favorite part of Scotland. Searching the old ruins and museums there I picked up my desire for all things old and antique.

Several years ago Eileen was so excited to show us a new car lot in Ayr. We were both not so sure how a car lot could be interesting. We said nothing but a car park was not new to us from The United States.

When we arrived and saw it was a parking lot structure on the backstreet two stories high, we looked at each other and did mention we have had them in the USA since we were little girls.

They were in love with it but I understood because there was so much old here, and nothing to compare it to, made it a big moment.

We had parked and were walking towards the main street when all of a sudden I felt a touch on my cheek. Looking quickly at Elaine I saw she was intent on the stores so I interrupted "something touched my cheek Elaine, did you see anything, like maybe the wind was blowing leaves or anything?" She simply shook her head and we went on.

I thought about it all afternoon. It had a soft touch and my cheek actually felt warm for a second or two. I remembered when I began to ask Elaine, who was Eileen's daughter not my sister, Eileen's daughter, when a wind blew towards us,we hurried. It rains almost everyday in Scotland. So we had to hurry.

The afternoon went by quickly and we hurried back to EIleen's home.When we got there we had a great big surprise waiting for us.'Come in ladies I have made plans for your evening. Eileen told us.

"Bob's Mother has invited you to dinner and to spend the night there with her and her husband."

"She remembered you a few years ago when you told her you didn't believe in ghosts, but wanted to see one or experience a haunting, sometime in your life.She continued, knowing I loved ghosts.

"First of all The house was haunted. I first learned about it when I met Bob and after his Mom told me the stories that Bob did actually confirm..Behind her little house in the field had been a Monastery mabe 300 years ago, maybe the 16th century, and she can tell you some scary stories that happened to them. I know you will love it."The excitement was unbearable and I could not stop talking about it.

Bob's great,great,great grandfather had taken the liberty of moving some of the stones from the old monastery, after hundreds of years, and they had crumbled into a pile of rocks, and brought them up towards the little cobbled street where they built a small home. They eventually had two children, Bob and a sister.

Bob had already spoken to us about the house. Telling us scary things that we both thought he was making up.He wasn't!

Each year we went antique hunting in some obscure place in Scotland, old Monasteries, and Ruins. At first it was only myself traveling, then I talked Elaine into coming with me.

When Bob was a kid he told us, there were chickens clucking all through the night. His Mom had explained that she heard it too. But there were no chickens anywhere near the house they lived in. It was a lonely country road, one lane only, and only their home. And notmany other homes nearby, so they had no one to compare their stories to at the time.

40 years before he was born his mothers sister had been killed in front of this old home, a horse drawn cart had run loose and ran over her and she had died. The story she told us that night was so frightening and hard to believe, but she spoke of it with knowledge that only a little girl who had been there could have had.

Bob's mother, who I called Gran, had also told us that she had taken a cutting of her sister's hair and a piece of her dress and the ribbon in her hair and made a doll. This doll was sitting on the bed she gave to us. We went back down the stairs and asked her if that was the doll she had made? "Yes dearie" in that old Scotch Brogue, she replied, and at first mention of it, I had cold chills all over my body. Trying to be a nice person I dropped the subject. But when we got upstairs to go to bed I took the doll and wrapped it in a bath towel and stuffed it in the hamper in the hall.

We both did not sleep at all that night. We talked a lot then it was morning and we got dressed and went down the stairs.

Waiting for Eileen to pick us up was hard. We had had no sleep and wanted to leave. But we did not want to upset Gran. So we ate her breakfast that was so good. Then we talked a while and Eileen arrived to pick us up. We said thank you to Gran and when we left she invited us back but we both knew that was not going to happen again.

Also that night Gran had told us about her daughter who was a nurse and worked a shift ending at midnight, and she had always waited up for her to come home. Every night at midnight, Jane had walked down the flagstone short pebbled path to the side door, to her home, and there were so many times she would see a man dressed in all black from the hood on his cloak to his feet. He was walking past her mothers side door back towards where the Monastery had been three hundred years ago. She often told her mother about him, and so they had begun a new schedule for Jane, as she returned each night Gran waited outside the door, with her umbrella, when she heard her arrive,then opening this door she stood outside and she would let her in. Gran told us she had seen the black monk many times but didn't dwell on it..

Gran said she had wanted to tell them she had seen him many times before but had chosen not to dwell on those many times she had seen one or more of these very big black figures walking back towards the land where the monetary had been three hundred years before they built their house...

Remembering the very low price they had gotten when searching for a parcel of land to build on, I had a good idea why no one else would want it.

She told us one night her husband had gone to bed before she did and when she walked upstairs to their room she was shocked when she turned into the room. In this tiny room their bed had been moved right in the doorway. She woke him up and asked him why he moved the bed, but he told her he did not move it at all, the "Big Mon"moved it.

After that she had tried to make him understand she had heard nothing, and when you move furniture that heavy it would take three men. She told us he never changed his story in all the years after, and until he died.

Elaine, their daughter, was not at all scared after hearing these stories but made sure we did not sleep in that room.

That night the only thing we heard were the chickens that were not there.Ha Ha, oh yes they were. Loud and clear we heard them all night long.

That was enough. We chose not to stay there after that, but we did visit the sweet old lady, each year.

When Eileen picked us up that morning we had a few laughs but when we told her the chickens clucked all night she just smiled and shook her head as if to say yes I told you so. We all laughed for a long time then drove back to Ayr where we had left the rental car.

After we all had an Indian Meal at our favorite place Ayr India, we went back to Eileens to pack up because tomorrow we were leaving for London and then our real vacation would begin. The Antiques were on our mind as we said goodbye and made sure we were invited back soon.

Driving down Lamford Drive out of Doonbank Estates, heading to Glasgow for our short flight to London we both were very excited for the antiques we were going to search out today.

The flight was only 45 minutes and smooth as I hoped the rest of our day went. Although it was going to be a challenge today, we had no idea yet.

CHAPTER 9

After we checked into the hotel we both headed out to the street to get a cab to the antique district. One place we both loved and knew by heart.

"I know we are going to have a fun day Elaine, somehow today, I have a funny feeling here, I'm sure today you might find your Suit of Armor."smiling I headed down a new street I had not been on before, but I had heard a lot of talk of Wick. The last thing she said to me before we got separated "See you at three sister"Elaine called out to me as she hurried down the small street.

Have you ever felt the tingling in your feet when they just would not go fast enough for you?

Today was one of those days for me. "Excuse me sir"I said as I almost ran over the small man in front of me. He turned and said "better to be there in one piece than hurrying and losing your way and not finding what it is I feel is also waiting near for you". I turned and smiled and thought whatever you idiot, and hurried on. Later on I had time to remember his warning and his strange words to a stranger.

I could feel it pulling me, but I had no idea what"It was"I was being led to at the moment. Slowly seeing a red and green awning in front of me about three more stores down the way, I got there and realised I hadn't seen this one before.

Standing out in front I felt a happiness going over me like rain falling. But no it was not raining,I reached to open the large glass door but it opened for me. There was a lady there holding the door open. "Good morning Mam" she called as I walked in and quickly I felt like a homing pigeon.

"Why hello to you too Mam,.I feel as though I may have seen this shop even though I have been on this street many times, but I don't remember it at all."But I realized there were quite a few antiquities here that I felt was a good thing for me.I am looking for a special Grandfather clock and it will be very old and the wood will be very dark brown, with the glass all glittering with sequins in between the layers of glass."She laughed and asked, ``How long will you be in London?"As if she knew me. I said avoiding her question as if I did not even hear her, "My sister and I are also on a search for a very very old particular Suit Of Armor that she saw in Berlin a while ago, we researched it in depth but we did not find the one she wants. It has red spots of paint in many different places."Circa approximately 1408 Knights -- Suit of Armor. We know it did exist but the dating goes back before there were many records, hence making it very difficult to locate even a photo let alone more information.

My sister has a photo of the one she hopes to find, and it is not very clear, but clear enough that she knew immediately it was the one she wanted. She found that photo in an old brown beat up box of things that were on the street to be picked up by the trash truck, several years ago, and it is the exact one she has been looking for many years, for this armor. When she saw that photo her heart spoke to her saying "Here I am"she gently touched my sleeve and I turned back to see what she wanted, and her face had a painful look, so I immediatley touched her hand to ask if she was ok, when she turned and pointed to the trash bin on the street. Pointing her finger my eyes traveled to the photo laying there face up, it was easy to see that it had been a treasured photo of someone at one time maybe centuries ago, because it still had a side of the gold gilt frame on it, gold gilt in my opinion. Reaching down I saw the glass was broken and parts of this photo were wet and distorted, maybe not plain as day, but there it was her Suit Of Honor, the same one she had talked about since we were kids and played with the boys up the street. Her face was crumpled. I could tell she saw more than I saw but there was no conversation about this faded old, crumpled photo taken who knows where or when. Needless to say she rescued it for her treasure in part.

"This will go home with me and then when we travel I will always have the photo and the hope in my heart that someone will recognise it, and have some information that we can track down and check it out, even if it is the wrong one I will keep my hopes up.

I changed the subject then and we turned back toward another shop. I was hoping to get this off her mind until we returned to our room where I was already beginning to imagine the conversation I dearly wanted to have with her.

I saw the deserted look in her eyes as they traveled from one corner of that old photo to another side.

She was lost in the photo is what I kept telling myself as the long minutes dragged on. We had discussed this Suit Of Armor many times but in my mind I never had a clear vision of what she was saying. On the other hand she knew exactly what she was looking for.

I remember asking her how she came up with this idea and she said point blank as if I should already know the answer, and I saw the love in her eyes or was it hope?

"The dream"do you remember when we were very young and the night I screamed, and you tried to wake me up and ran down stairs to get Mamma, when I wouldn't stop crying"?It was then the memories came rushing back, and I remembered something about her telling Mamma she had a dream and there was a man in a silver metal outfit staring into her eyes. She said her heart was beating so fast and she was afraid.

Our Mother would sit down beside her and hold her in her arms until she quieted down. I'm not sure if she even told Daddy about the dreams because they seemed far apart and just a little girl's dreams. The soothing sweet voice we had grown up loving so much all the days of our life.

CHAPTER 10

When we were a little older we found out our Mother had been adopted. We had asked many questions and she so patiently answered all that she knew the answer to. But she had not much information at all. Her adoptive Mother, our grandmother whose name was Ruby, had told her very little and she grew up in a very affluent family, and had wanted to forget that, because she always said to us that she so very lucky because she had been picked out from among many orphans st that time in the orphanage. She was the very best Mother any little girls could have ever wanted. And we both knew it. When we compared our mother to our friends Mothers there was always something lacking that we both felt, and we knew these other friends did not have it as lucky as we did, hands down the Best.

The little book seemed to be getting warmer and it almost felt hot in my pocket. I took it out to see why it felt so hot. And believe me it was hot to the touch.

This lost feeling had made me think about more questions. During all this time I was still walking and searching for the way out,looking for any way out. I never said the word lost but my brain was very smart and I knew I was seeing things and places that I had not seen before.

I looked at my Apple watch and it was getting very late. Feeling really disoriented, I saw a couch in the corner and as my last resort took a seat. Trying to calm myself down and make some sense of this I looked all around. I was feeling very tired by now, and my eyes seemed to want to close, and even as I told myself I needed to have my wits about me, I really was confused, and so I tried to settle down and closed my eyes just for a minute. Or so I thought.

Beginning to feel sleepier. It seemed like time was passing, and then I guess I went to sleep, because when I opened my eyes again there was light, and there was a feeling of peaceful happiness coming over me.I checked to make sure I still had the book, then I decided to find my way out of this place. Looking around I was surprised to find that I was not in the Antique Shop anymore.

And this was more a shock than anything else, trying to make sense of this I began to walk around and check out the surroundings. All I wanted was to find the door and then head straight to the hotel to let Elaine know I was fine. Even as I thought that, something in my head said "no you are not alright girl".

Then I thought I saw the sun shining in the back of a room, and headed towards it. It was then the book in my hands got hot again. Weird enough. So not entirely forgetting the book, I held it up to the light source and it was telling my brain to go on out into the light. And I began to walk as if my brain always did things like this.

Even knowing everything I saw was so wrong, I kept on walking. Talking to myself was not an option right now.

Eyes wide open I walked more. But then I remembered my Mommy asking her questions, and trying to get some answers because this was not the first time she had had this dream, but maybe the fourth time. She would scream and shake for hours after we woke her up, so it was something our mother tried to get out of her mind whenever she said that the man was not real but all metal with eye openings. I had seen my mother look around the room and hold her fingers up to her face as if she was trying to remember or place when my sister could have seen anyone dressed like that. The description was all metal with the face mask and two eye openings. This seemed to be the most information she ever got from her, except one night she said blood was all over him and she was trying to wash it off of herself in the dream. And so that had to be where the red came into the picture.

Whenever we talked about it Elaine would say the red spots were on it, which we finally decided had to have been blood.

Elaine always said, after every dream, that he had his hand out, and was always there and always trying to pull her away from our bed and take her with him. And when she asked him where he was taking her, that's when he changed the subject and wanted to know why her mother tried to make him go away and she told her mother what he said, and our sweet smart Mother cried. The thoughts that her cute baby girl who was now about eight years old broke her heart. After this happened many times she felt she needed to get to the bottom of the horrible dream, one so bad her baby girl could not shake it for very long before it came again. Trying everything she could think of, nothing worked.we noticed she tried to keep us so busy that when we went to bed we were worn out. Nothing was going to stop this and I guess she knew it and decided to deal with it when it came.

That was about the time when I started to dream about her Suit Of Armor and the blood marks, and the man she said was inside it. As the years went by we tried to forget about it but she never forgot the dreams, but I did for a time.

Our Mother found things for us to do and it helped both of us to push it out of our minds. Things.

Changed, like we wanted to have a Circus in the backyard and grow our own flower gardens filled with Zinnia's that Daddy dug up for us each summer.

And Marigolds. I remember they smelled so bad...

All these years later the memories came back and that's when we both talked about an article we saw in the newspaper about the unusual items in a nearby Yard sale. This started us traveling abroad, after a while, searching for these things we wanted, but we soon found they were not out there. Then we studied the computer for ideas. It soon became a favorite thing to do together.

Often on the other hand we would give up on her dream and concentrate on my dream. I was also looking for a very old Grandfather Clock, and I had also seen it in a photo in the encyclopedia one day as I was browsing and looking at all the old Grandfather Clocks I could rummage up. But of course I did not see the one I was hoping to find..'The one I want is from 1448.....how did I come up with that date? I really only remembered in my mind someway, it, but how or why there was not an answer to that then.

What were the chances I'd ever find or read about this Clock? I always hoped Elaine and I would find our treasures someday and never thought of forgetting the dreams. Really in my mind I knew the answer and it was "probably"never. But hope is always there...

Conversation ended. I took the opportunity, and I walked away to search through all these old beautiful things I remember looking behind me, with the feeling there was someone there following me. But nothing and no one was there. In the far back left hand of this dark old store I saw a man who appeared to be looking at me! He began walking toward me. Chills rushed over my body and the closer he got the colder I felt. Walking around a corner thinking he was leaving did not work. "Excuse me Mam," he said as he bent his head and removed his hat. The entire sentence sounded like he had been practicing, but now he looked at me and said "I have been waiting for you."

"I beg your pardon but I have no idea who you might be. As you can probably tell I'm an American and we have never met before, of that I am sure.

If you don't mind I was on my way out, excuse me, And then I tried to get around him without ever getting too close.

As I tried to get around him he seemed to be stepping in my way on purpose. "Oh dear me Mam I did not mean any disrespect, but I do know that you are in search of a certain GrandFather Clock, I believe the one you search for is Polish made, maybe the age will be about 1336 and stands in the "Mysterious Antiquities"about three streets over. Am I right?"

I really didn't know who he was or why he had spoken to me. I just stared at him and said I was sorry. He was a pure gentleman of that I was now sure. Don't ask me how, it just came into my mind that he looked a lot like my Grandaddy.

Speechless I just nodded my head and could not think of a word to say. Then I told him, "thank you so much sir."

He seemed so confident. So sure. But I finally said, as I was walking out "Look sir I appreciate your thinking that you know of me, and how you know what I am searching for, but I do not know you and although you seem to know me I'm sure you don't sir, walking I kept looking back, I said, "so thanks"again but I have to leave now.

I turned and almost ran out of the old shop. Never looking behind me. I felt like I heard his words echoing in my ears. But, never looking back I continued to my hotel, hoping Elaine was there so I had someone to talk to and this story was something to tell! thanking God, she was there, thank God!

CHAPTER 11

As soon as I entered our room, I felt the tension leave my body. I went straight to my bed and curled up on the pillows planning in my mind how to tell Elaine.She always believed me no matter what odd thing came up.

Together we had seen a lot of strange things as we hunted the allys on our trips.

Settling down on the cushions on my bed, I crossed my legs and said,"You will not believe this when I tell you about a man who I ran into in the Antiquities shop next door to the shop with the blue door.."

I was out of breath and I could feel my legs still shaking and there was a strange feeling of fear in my brain, that I did not recognise..through all our searching and traveling I did not remember anything like I was feeling today. "Calm down"and Elaine said, I'm waiting and Im disturbed to see you in this fear mode. What did the man do to you?"Elaine asked me, and I thought maybe I looked worse than I thought I did. So I went through the episode telling one thing then another until I had her complete attention.

"Sister, what do you think it meant when he approached you and asked you about your search, then proceeded to tell you what it was you were looking for. "Are you sure you didn't tell him?"

I could see the look on her face. "How strange, and it is also more than a little out of the norm, and scary, and very bizarre " Please, (pointing to the chair), sit down and calm yourself. There is a bottle of expensive Sherry on the table, and I know we don't usually drink alcohol of any kind, but Let me get us both a glass of Sherry. The maids will think we got drunk after all when they come in and have to replace the complimentary bottle." Then let's get this story straight.""I said, trying to change the subject, because I did not he found this information, and how did this man act as if he already knew these things about me?"

After a sip or two I felt myself calming down. Looking at Elaine I was trying to think how to tell this because it was so disturbing to say the least.

"Elaine, I can't tell you what a strange man he was. But I took it very seriously that he thought he knew my business and or my mind, how?I do not have any idea".

Just lookin at with both her beautiful manicured hands, under her chin, resting on the table in front of her. I could tell she wanted some answers but how could.

"Well now that you are back, let's pick up where we were before you saw this crazy old man. First of all you do remember that we made a pact to never get separated and always stay close to each other in these antique Markets,"We need to stay together and keep in touch when we are out there in Antique Ville. We sometimes have to go our own way, and I'm already forgetting about him. Remember what we came here for"she looked at me to make sure I was ok, "we will meet back up at 4:30, does that sound like we have enough time to investigate some of these shops? Smiling, my mind was good now so we walked out of our room together.

I went out the door and stood there for a few minutes as Elaine pointed across the street, and said come on, when she waved to meI started to have a chill. Shaking my arms I thought to myself "whatever was that about and then my ears were ringing, then I shook my head and turned around, heading somewhere but having no place in mind at the moment, of course I was going to stay close to her wherever she headed....

CHAPTER 12

Thinking about going down to all those older shops in Covent Gardens made me happy again. The Greenwich Market was next on my list, I turned and retraced my steps, heading to the one where I felt so much turmoil when I first walked in. I felt it pulling me again. I waved at Elaine and pointed to the building I wanted to go into, and she nodded yes, she would follow me in free minutes, there was something in the store in front of her that she wanted to check out first. I shook my head yes and pointed again to the Blue door. She smiled and I went in.

The chill was still there. So I put my arms around my body and rubbed down my arms. As soon as I felt the chill going I started to glance around and saw a flash of light down the block of shelves to my right, then I had the chill again, so I thought that maybe I better be on my way, hoping I was not getting sick. Sick was the only thing I could think of that would make me feel like this.

A brand new feeling of being sick flashed into my head, what a bother I was thinking. Walking on I saw where it was coming from. Flash's bouncing off the building and straight to my eyes.

About a block away I had a feeling that said to me.

"Here I am so come on, I'm waiting"Shaking my head as if I could make it go away, only made me look retarded, and seeing people looking my way then ducking their head as if I had not seen them, go off in another direction.

Standing there thinking the worst thoughts ever, I shook my head again and started walking.

Again I heard a voice, "look straight ahead, do you feel it?

My whole body was chilled by now. Where was Elaine when it looked like I needed her support to tell me stop-it! But...she was across the street and I knew it.

I was laughing, because I thought maybe that wine was too much for me in the middle of the day. Walking straight ahead all of a sudden I had a hot feeling and then my legs started to tingle. First chilled and now hot oh my word was all I could think. I kept walking because I didn't know why I was having these strange feelings, I figured maybe I needed to get back to our room, as soon as possible, and it was ahead a couple of streets.

Walking but not concentrating on the area in front of me, all of a sudden and I had no idea where I was.

Knowing London side streets were not at all familiar. Leaning against a piece of a short post, I felt strange, as though I was going to faint. At once I knew I had to try to locate our hotel so I could just give up shopping today and go to our room. It had already proved to be not my day.

Wherever Elaine was shopping I knew she would come to the room sooner or later, or try calling the cell phone when she was ready to leave. Of course I was assuming she was still shopping.

CHAPTER 13

As I walked the way I supposed our hotel should be, all of a sudden, I felt very light headed and then I felt a chill coming out of the door beside me.

I had had enough of this strange chilling feeling and DeJa Vous.... Wow really!!.

Rubbing both my arms to stop the chill I thought I could maybe stop this feeling. And then it was happening all over again, a male voice whispering in my ears or maybe my brain?

I heard his voice in my ears, but saw no one that would always prove to be ridiculous.

And then looking at storefronts I had never seen before. And with it the feeling that I had to go in, was overwhelming. Where was Elaine right now.?

Why we had not stayed together was a question I would be asking myself for a very long time.

"Hello," Said a very familiar voice, this time speaking directly to me, but in my mind I kept thinking that I was too smart to be having these feelings, and with sounds too, if they were not really there.

"Come on in, when I saw you were close, I had to speak out to you."Said the very deep voice….

"My name is Domangus"he said bowing to me.

So Far no one had ever bowed to me before. What a creep I thought, turning to go back where I came from.

Glancing around myself, I saw I was all by myself, and the door I entered from was not there now…. What in the world is a name like that I wondered? In my mind I was saying "Oh hello Damangus"A huge smile on my face.

So I stepped inside and oh my goodness, the first coherent thought I had was, it was freezing in there. Looking for this man who called himself Domangus, was impossible in the dark atmosphere of this store I was in. Testing the dark floor I walked a few steps and then all of a sudden, I felt faint. I knew it was time for me to leave now and quickly.

"Rubbing my forehead, blinking my eyes to establish some surroundings, I realized I had no idea where I was. Or what time it was. Here I was walking on a very hard floor, each step echoing, that possibly went nowhere, and it was so very dark, and then I felt myself falling down.

It finally dawned on me that I must have passed out, because this had to be a dream or what some normal people might have called a nightmare!

And why did I feel lost, even though my mind told me "You just walked in", it was because I had no recognition of my surroundings at all. As I tried to remember and kept going back in my mind to pull pieces to help, it did not go well at all...

Maybe one minute later, I felt a hand at my elbow, trying to help me up. But I really saw no one, just the helping hands of someone in this dark room.. I could not help thinking someone was there to help me, and it really did make sense.I followed the arm in the dark and then I came into light that I saw coming from a fireplace. Staring around me I suddenly had a shiver rush through my whole body.

"I Am here to help you,"I heard the voice coming again from my right elbow area. Turning my head I saw I was in a chamber like none other I had ever seen. There were rows of black ribbon like a snake maybe, going from the floor to the ceiling in different and trimmed with the most beautiful handcrafting I had ever seen before. Like a really dark tunnel. I was trying to figure out how hard it must have been to arrange this.

Also wondering what kind of place I was in? I was so miserable, and everything was moving so slow. Or so I thought, "Hello I said"then out of nowhere a very bright light was building up to my far right. I stared, not just a light but yes it was a distant sparkling light series.

It appeared spark-like, then all around me I felt and saw the flame was building brighter. Because we had just arrived, where jet lag had not been bad at first but maybe it just took hold of me later, I really was worrying now."Hello,"I spoke again, still not an answer.

No one answered my hello. No one answered at all, and as I struggled and got to a standing position, I was trying hard to see in the distance, it was just so dark. And all of a sudden it was like my wish was coming true, oh Dear God, there He was. Really it was…My Dream in front of my eyes.!

It was there…my hearts dream` OMG, The Grandfather Clock, of my dreams.

All shiny and beautiful to my eyes. Of course this had to be a shot in the dark but again, I thought.

So I was dreaming, I was so sure.

But as I started to walk towards the Grandfather clock I could actually feel it pulling me, actually dragging me, because my legs wouldn't work. "Is there anyone here? Can you please turn on some sort of light for me?"

Nothing at all did I hear. And at the moment Elaine was not here, and I suddenly realized how much I needed her, so I was alone but here I was looking at my dream Clock.

All I could think, was where is Elaine and what will Elaine think when I don't come back to our room,

In this dark I could not see two feet in front of me. And I knew my Clock was there. So I put my arms out trying to touch the space I was in and whatever I could find to steady myself and tried to walk around a little bit, shaking my head to try to clear my vision. Then I just found some sort of a chair beside me, and felt I had to sit down, before I fell down.

Sitting there lost as a girl could be, I think I fell asleep after the first few minutes went slowly by, and trying not to think at all I suddenly knew I was close to falling asleep. I was just overwhelmed with the thought of Elaine, and where she was.With a last look around at my dark surroundings I was just so darn sleepy and then nothing!

CHAPTER 14

Time passed and I began to wake up, and I grew aware of the space I was sitting in. Artifacts staring me in the eyes. Remembering where I was did not work, my memories were sketchy. Closing my eyes; Not one thought came to me.

Nothing absolutely nothing was there when I opened my eyes this time. I guess I was going to have to go along with the ride. Wherever the ride will take me.

Where I was headed I had no idea, so not seeing much in the dismal lighting here I slowly tried to stand up, moving my feet one in frontof the other.

Expecting who knows what, and I kept moving even as I held on to anything I could grasp, I still felt a kind of a fear settling in my heart. Prior to this feeling I had never ever felt a cold fear like this one it was all over me and my brian was on alert, I did not know what or why but weird was the word.

I found myself trying to scrutinize the area where I was, looking for information of any kind. There was nothing in particular to see but a chair in a corner, and the fireplace that was burning brighter with each minute, I decided just to go over and sit in that chair and try to gather my wits about myself. In the distance, I thought I heard the voice of the man who had spoken to me in the Antiquities store earlier.

Deciding to sit still and wait for the next sound and then to try to make a clear decision on my next move.

"Hello," I said very loudly. The answer was the same voice, so I said "can you tell me what is going on here please sir, I remember your voice and I saw you in another store a while ago."

There was the sound of his movement somewhere close to where I was sitting. I was totally frightened. A few seconds later the lighting grew brighter, and I saw him with matches in his hand.

"So it's you" I said in a depressed sort of voice. He seemed to be staring at something in the corner. So I looked that way to see the Grandfather Clock I had been dreaming about for years. There were little tiny lights flying all around the face of the clock. I blinked my eyes several times but each time I opened them I could still see the lights. They seemed to be fading. I turned to look at the man who was still standing there. I wondered if he saw the lights too. I waited a second or two, still no mention of the blinking. Eventually I turned to see if there were any other people in the antique shop. I saw something. But it was too dark to recognise anything here at the moment.

`My mind was in shock. Seeing the clock with my own eyes made me happy, my heart was skipping beats, but also fear went with it. Deciding to sit still and rest, I made a mental note to revisit that Grandfather Clock in the corner, as soon as I felt all this emotion disappear, hopefully in a few minutes, and I needed to see Him safely. Oh my Goodness I had called the clock by a masculine name. What was going on in my brain right now.

I felt better in a very few minutes and decided to venture toward the clock that I felt was calling me continuously. Now Shaking my head and looking all around the darkened room to see if there was someone there who was speaking to me, I was reassured that I was totally alone. Absolutely alone.

Standing up feeling queasy I stood still for a couple of minutes. Then, when I felt like I could walk over there, I looked for something close to hold on to as if I might need it. I was feeling pretty steady and so as I looked ahead of me, it felt like something was needing my attention, but it was ever so clear to my fuzzy mind at the same time, there was no one anywhere.. Reaching out in the dim lighting, to feel the huge fluffy armchair I could see, I stood still, then I began to move straight.

It took my very last breath away at first.

I walked all the way around him. Looking at each beautiful side and decoration, from side to side, from the top to the bottom, the details were embedded in my mind and my memory Suddenly it became much clearer.

Suddenly, there was a long glass door, and it was so deep, and so wide and in the bottom there was a space, like an empty area someone might store something in there. and it was speaking to my mind as clearly as if there was a person standing there. In my mind I thought I heard the I shook my head, stretched my arms then put my mind back on the most beautiful Clock I had ever envisioned.

There it was again, "Open me up now"I heard it and felt it. Plain as if someone was standing beside me. I heard it. But my brain knew there was no one there that could speak. I remembered rubbing my forehead and saying to myself in my mind, "this clock cannot speak".

But still the voice was there. So I walked a little closer and reached out my right hand to the handle. I was surprised because the Grandfather clocks of today had a key hole and no handle. The handle felt warm in my hand. It made me smile. My brain was saying why are you smiling. But I really was so happy. As I carefully opened the shimmering glass door, there was a chill in the air, and I felt it all over my body.I rubbed the chills that appeared on my arms, then bent over to see closer the chimes. They were so beautiful, appearing to be brass or silver. They were more beautiful than any I had ever seen in my searching, and I had seen so many through the years of looking for my clock. Oh how I wanted to touch them. Then, out of the corner of my eye, and on the floor of the clock, I saw a little square object in the bottom on the floor of the clock. As I bent over and reached in, the dizziness returned. Shaking my head to clear the fuzziness and planning to get my thoughts together, I realized that what I was seeing was a small book, maybe a diary? Although it was very dark in here I saw it clearly, ragged and torn and moldy and then I was reaching in for it. I wondered when I Got so brave and at last my heart said. "Go ahead."

Or maybe my brain spoke those words to me.

So I took the book in my hands, and immediately I felt something stinging on my fingers. Shaking my arms and laying the little old worn brown book down, the sensations left me. Seeing it laying there I felt like I was lost and I needed it in my hands now.

By now I was really feeling shaky again, shaking my head hard. I finally picked the little book up and held it to my chest and then walked toward a chair I saw in front of me. Holding it near to my heart I felt a sadness pass through my head. Sitting down, I thought I was going to cry, but why I did not know.

Now making myself comfortable I opened the pages of the book very, and the fragile pages were almost hard to read so I was very careful of the book. I became really worried that if I let anything happen to the treasure I would be responsible and it was probably worth a fortune if not ten fortunes...

I laid it gently in my lap and looked about me to see if anyone had seen me open the old fragile glass door, or if anyone had seen the lights I first saw. It seemed that there was no one else there but me. I stood up and spoke up loudly, "is there anyone here"but no one was there. I tried to see if there was anything, something, anything I remembered from my walk towards the clock.

The only person around was me. Looking everywhere, I knew I had seen nothing familiar when I walked into the old Anti.

At the moment I had forgotten about Elaine. Feeling so sure she was back at our hotel and safer than I was at the moment. And the thought of going back to our hotel was never in my thoughts at this time. All that was on my mind was the little book warm in my hands. Wondering if I could read it and worrying that if I was not careful, I would destroy my book, in the fragile condition it was in. I was shaking all over, my hands and my arms were trembling. I knew it was my book...

My next move was to try to find somewhere I could sit down and protect this treasure and read some entries into my book, while thinking about it. I was holding it gently to my heart.

Realizing it might look weird to see a grown woman holding an antique book so close to my heart, like a treasure, I hung my arms down and I tried to relax and walked toward the front door. But there was no front door.

I was really sure now that I was in a mess. So looking all around, it seemed that this was not where I came in, and nothing looked the same as I remembered it. I realized I could not remember anything, not a single fragment of the past few moments and finding the book that I already felt was mine.

Right now I am really scared. Imagining what people might think of me under these circumstances.

A grown woman on a trip to England goes antique searching and finds a treasure in a beautiful old Shop. Still looking and turning around I did not see an exit anywhere. Shaking a little bit I found another chair and walked toward it, I sat down. Carefully laying the book in my lap, All at once I realized I was beginning to feel very tired. The next instant I was tucking the diary under my shirt, the next thing I remembered was closing my eyes, my fear came back, and then the dream took over again.

I did not fight it but went with it, and kept my hands around my secret little book I had found.

It began, this crazy dream, and I saw nothing familiar, but then I saw a young woman sitting under a tree full of pink blossoms blowing in the distance. She was also in pink, with a huge straw hat covered with flowers, to keep the sun off her face. I felt I had seen this before. It felt too familiar to me, I thought maybe it was mine?

Not possible, I knew in real time. But what time was this? Suddenly I knew I was not even sure what time It was now, and not too sure where I really might be.

I stood very still and looked all around me to find something familiar, but everything I saw was new to me. I was worrying while I wondered where I was.I saw there was a lake in front of me,, there were so many trees with blossoms on them, and the ducks swimming in the lake were making sounds. I told myself this was a dream but when I pinched myself I felt it. Feeling the book in my hands it reminded me I needed to find Elaine to bring her up to date.and I wanted to return to our room.

But how? My brain said "you can do that but how?"This was not the time for frightened thinking.

I had to get back inside that shop, and out the front door, to my sister. Elaine's fear when I didn't show up was more than I could imagine, if the situation was reversed this thought was not what I wanted to unravel. My sister's welfare and safety was the most important option. I was the one who talked her into coming on this journey, since we both loved antiques.

After all, we had been on a long journey just three months before, so when I found this auction of fine old antiques and never being there before I begged her to come.

Up to today everything was going great. But now I cannot say that anymore. Not right now anyway. I could not say anything because I had to be dreaming and I was so lost. This was not possible. I knew the way I came into this shop, but it was so dark, and I was actually lost, and that was not me,

Elaine and I knew our way around any place we might land in, never ever once being lost.

Thinking about the word lost, I realized the risk of being found here was at an all time low. Looking around I thought "ok just where am I?

When I tried to turn around to see which way out was closest, I was surprised to find no exit signs at all. And I reminded myself I wanted to make an offer on the Clock before I left. My mind was in a jumbled mess.And at the same time I was looking for an exit.

All at once I was outside in the beautiful sunlight.

It was a pleasure to see the light of day and to be out of that old dusty musty smelling shop.

Then all at once I was thinking and realized Elaine had been alone all night and I started to feel very nervous because she would have had no idea where I was. We were always so careful to never leave the other one alone without explicit mention of where and what time to meet.

And more than that, this time I absolutely didn't know where I was.

Then my brain spoke up. Wherever I was, I didn't have a clue. Looking all around me when everything else was becoming scary, I held the warm book to my heart. I was thinking maybe I had died. But pinching myself hurt so, no I knew I was alive.

I had no idea what to do next, so I found a spot in the direct sunshine and sat down. Holding my book in my hands I knew what I was about to do, I was going to read the beginning of this book.

I was sure Elaine was already looking for me so I Did not give it a single thought again.

The first page was worn and looked like it had been read a hundred times already. I leaned back and then I saw the inscription that said:

"please help me I have been stolen from my family and I am writing in this book that I found in the crevices of an old Grandfather Clock, it had been in our out building and no one really wanted it, because I had seen the old clock there for maybe three years, all dirty and no one ever mentioned it...I assumed that it was a relic no one wanted anymore. It couldn't be a family thing since I had never seen it in any home before,

I shook it hoping it would chime but no it wouldn't I thought, ``So here is the perfect place to put my diary."I have been locked away for a few years now, no one knows I have my diary. So I sneak outside in the late evening to write my desirs and I pray that someone finds it and comes to my rescue. Days go by and every day I wait to see someone show up to rescue me but nothing happens. I have been held here captive for a long time now, with no hope left, of ever being rescued. I was sure my parents were killed in the raid from marauding Vikings who landed at our pier late one evening.

I was sitting on the sandy beach writing in this journal when I saw the big colorful flags blowing in the wind as the ship came into sight. I tried to run to tell my family they were landing but I had not gotten any closer to my home when I heard them running after me. I only hope now that someone finds this diary and rescues me. I pray every day as I sit here in my tiny corner watching through a tiny hole a mouse could get through, that someone will rescue me. But as the days go by I feel like there is not much hope left in me for being rescued. I pray every day to be found. And I pray to keep my sense about me until the day comes and I am rescued from here."It is so hard to go back and relive all these horrible memories.

CHAPTER 15

I remember being grabbed from behind and tied up securely and then I was tossed into a huge wooden barrel on their ship and I could barely breathe, if I had not found the holes with big plugs in them, I would certainly be dead.

Knocking these cork type plugs out, so I could get a breath of fresh air. I knew what I must do, finally I saw light and felt the air coming in and I could breathe again, but I knew it was too late to warn anyone and soon I could smell the fires burning, and heard the screams from people in my home as they were targeted. As my heart and mind took all of this in I began to panic, I knew to be quiet or I would be the next one they killed. I curled up into a knot and made no sound. I prayed for my mother and father and two brothers to be able to escape.

When all the noise became quiet again, and I felt the ship rocking, and no one came down where I was hiding, I knew I had little chance of escaping these Viking murderers, so I stayed where I was and did not make a sound for many hours.

It must have been early in the morning when I awoke and there had been no one down here in the dark spaces around that I saw, So I sneaked fully out of the barrel, because I had been way down inside it, being as quiet as I could be, because the ships steps such as they were, were creaking loudly, and then all of a sudden, I heard them waking up and fear tore in to my brain, the next thought I had was to hide in a better spot before they all came back on board. Crawling around on my knees quietly I must have gone from one end to the other, and it was a long way, and then right in front of me I saw my chance to hide.

The huge old, old, looking clock from the outbuilding that I had seen a million times, and it had somehow been brought on board and stowed here in a dark and dirty corner of the crawl space, covered with spider webs and filth, I was in.As I got closer I saw it was the Grandfather clock from my home, or rather from the out building where it had been placed so many years ago. And it was so beautiful, even with all the dirt and mud and rocks around it. Quietly I moved closer until I could reach the dirty glass door. It was a huge clock, so huge, and the door opened easily for me. It was then I heard people groaning and moaning and being sick over the side of the boat. I tiptoed to the other side of the clock and tried to open the dirty painted door.To my shock it opened warmly and I felt like I was being invited to climb in.

I was shivering and so frightened that I could hardly move, looking all around I knew there was not much choice, but when the door fell open for some reason I stepped up and climbed into it. My body being so small just felt like it was home. It was a huge piece of furniture. My body being so small made it easy for me to see myself inside the glass door.I had never seen it up close before. The size made me think maybe it belonged to a giant!!

But never mind, I was hidden, and laying back against the warm wood I eventually fell asleep. It was so quiet and the boat was gently rocking me to sleep.

I'm sure I heard this conversation loud & clear while asleep, I was so scared that it felt not right to be here. Thinking about what I thought I heard, I went back over it again, and it always came out the same. These were murderers and they loved to kill people and watch them die.

"I am a tiny little Norwegian girl. My name is Scotia. If you are reading this please try to come rescue me from this horrible nasty smelling boat."There are mauraiding bad men everywhere. I seem to be smelling blood and the stench is bad. Scotia"

With such a scant amount of information I wondered for a very long time who this Scotia was. So it seemed only right, being in this situation that I assumed she was the person I was going to have to be. I was so nervous at first, and then these memories or whatever they were flew into my mind. I felt tears in my eyes at the picture of a little girl locked inside the Grandfather Clock.searching out the glass door. And the fact that it was the clock I was searching for made me feel passionate about Scotia's bad luck. I wanted to write or scratch a note saying, ``this is me and I need rescuing please."

I Just couldn't believe my mind when I tried to understand how this could be. And what I thought about, and how I had longed for and searched for this same particular clock, and that I was living this, what I thought of as a huge nightmare, at this moment in time, and I really wanted to wake up.

Sitting in the warm sunshine, feeling the warm rays reach into my body, I began to read the fragile pages, turning them one by one carefully. The words were reflecting back to me. I had no clue where I was or how I got there. I closed my most precious book, and put it in my pocket, carefully so I didn't tear any part of it.

Turning my head back and forth I saw the tall waving green grass and animals lazing in the warm sun. The boat was sitting still, and I was looking out this time because the Vikings were out hunting I guessed. Taking my chance I silently slid over the side and tried to swim to the shoreline making as little noise as possible...

CHAPTER 16

It was about an hour later, when I heard someone whistling, I knew that it was most certainly a man, somewhere behind me, as I stood up stretching my neck, looking around.

Seeing no one yet, I thought to walk towards the sounds. In the field ahead of me, I could see there were many strange looking animals. I thought maybe they were Buffalo, but then, maybe not, maybe the long red haired cattle grazing lazily in the beautiful warm sunshine were a different type of Buffalo. So then my brain said to me that I was thinking that I had to be in Scotland because these were surely long haired Highland cattle. So I turned to see the safest way to get myself out of harm's way and began to walk quickly and quietly to the nearest plank and wire twisted together with fencing. I saw that it was keeping these huge red hairy animals penned in. I counted twenty two huge ones. I knew if I Was quiet I was safe enough.

Again looking around and reaching the lowest spot in the fencing, that was open from a tear, that I could climb over, I could feel a huge relief that I was out of the way of those huge highland cattle just grazing in the field, that I woke up in, and thinking what could have happened if I had been trapped in this field without any way out was not something I should be thinking about, I was safe, even though I was lost, but there were people who thought they knew me seven though I had no idea who they were.

I was not too sure where I was, or what to do next. but these were cattle, maybe not buffalo, and then I knew the buffalo I had seen did not have that long shabby hair all over them. I began to believe they were highland cattle. If that was true I was still in England, or maybe Scotland.

Now as I looked away, I saw a man walking toward me. Then I heard another man somewhere in the same area, call him William?" Maybe at first it sounded like a question, I had thought, but no, I looked behind me but he was almost to me by now. I waited and he began to run to me, grabbing me up in the air like a dust rag, or toy, saying "Scotia"not a tiny girl like I was, then he hugged me.

Yes definitely, oh yes, I let him. The smile I felt on my face was the first smile in a long time, but still I did not really know who he was, even though I could tell by the look in his eyes, he thought he knew who I was. I was happy and at the same time fearful, but I kept thinking if he had hugged me that hard I instinctively knew he thought I was his Scotia, and wouldn't hurt me.

"Scotia where have you been?"he asked me, tears running from his eyes, and still shaking me.? I tried to ask him not to hold me so tight, and he let go of me.

Again I tried to speak, "Sir, I promise you, that is not my name."He stood still, looking at me, with questions on his face, that to me looked like, what was wrong? But I could tell he really thought I was Scotia, so I said what he wanted to hear, and yes of course, I spoke up with the words he was waiting for.

"What did you say?"I asked him, and noticed him

looking up at me, he reached to embrace me and rocked me back and forth. And I let him.

"Where have you been?' "We have been searching as far away as we could travel and praying for so long. For some tiny little clue to help us keep our faith that we would eventually find you, but no luck. Having no clue we were waiting for anything to come along, becoming our everyday lifestyle as we waited for you to show up, and waited everyday, for your safe return, we all gathered when we did not find your body"the crying continued for a long time and then he let me loose, and looking down at me he pasted a tiny smile on his face.It was when he took out this dirty looking hanky and wiped his eyes that I knew I was safe, for the moment.

But I could see the wretched lines about his blue eyes, and on his forehead as tried to let go of the terror they had all been living through since the day the Vikings had appeared on this island.

I was just so happy to be here, when they called it home. But, no, I was not Scotia.and no it wasn't home,But at the moment,. I was whoever they wanted me to be right now, and with the knowledge from the diary, I had to be smart and use it to my advantage. In my wildest thoughts, I could not imagine how this would play out if I had not found the diary, holding on to it close to my heart and being held so tight by a stranger was no easy task, but I was smart and I was going to use my knowledge to help me get through this.

I had to think quickly because the girl on the ship had to have been Scotia, and she evidently had belonged to this family. I hated to think that the real Scotia had been killed, I had no idea what to say so I hugged him and said "thank goodness"

I just started to walk and we walked until everything here reminded me of home."I then watched his face and felt like an actress simply acting out a movie on TV…

Taking my arm he said "come let me take you home so everyone can finally relax. The family you remember is not the same. Do you remember the Viking Raid on our property?"I shook my head yes.

Without a clue I played the part to the best of my feeble mind. But who was he? And even though I most certainly was not Scotia, I kept walking and trying to listen and storing this information was not easy. I slowed down a bit because I was so thirsty that I had to ask him how long before I could get a drink of water. He responded that my mother would have water for me and could we just walk a little bit further to meet up with them.

Finally as we got closer to the house, I saw that the land in front of my view was overrun with trees and wild bushes,and branches as if a terrible storm had hit there recently, mostly with thorns, and briars, and not even one fence to separate the pastures, or the animals, because all I could see was that all the animals were roaming together, and I was thinking how did these people live like this? There were knee high rock borders, with all kinds of vines and they were covered with black colored berries, and the other fruit I saw was growing on what I was sure they probably called fences. My brain was thinking about how these kinds of families, or people, decided what land was theirs and what was not. And so I came to the decision that it appeared that the wild look of this land was fitting, and these people did live like this, and as I kept walking down the hill, jumping over huge rocks, and finally ended up down by the ocean.

He was pulling me by the arm, and all I knew was, I had to be "Scotia"now. No matter how hard or what happened next I had to answer to Scotia. Little did I know she was going to be my saving grace.

As we came to the edge of the rough layered land, by a rock and board, and tin covered roof type shelter house, I saw people running out the small building, screaming her name. "Scotia"my mind was blown away for a time, but then I saw the tears and felt the arms holding me so very tight, like I would run away,

"Oh dear Lord you are back and safe,"she heard a woman's voice as she cried out the name Scotia, and saw her dropping to her knees, and folding her hands into a prayer.Crying and wringing her hands, as she spoke, "where have you been?Were you mistreated or hurt by the Vikings my love"this mother cried into her ear.

Leading me into the white stone rock house that looked like photos I had seen in magazines dating back to the Thirteenth Century, or maybe the Fourteenth, it was then I realized that my love of antiques was going to help me here.

I could use what I had learned from my Daddy here and put it to good use if I played the part until I really woke up or whatever the end might be.

Wherever here was at the moment. I certainly didn't know the answer to that question, and that also was hard on my mind. At long last I accepted what was in front of me at this moment in time.

So I went along with the play! Yes, so I was now, Scotia, and people were asking me questions that I had no answers for, but I remembered what I had read in the little paper book I had found, and repeated the things that I remembered. And I was so surprised, realizing thatIt had worked.

So as I played this part, things came and went into my brain. I felt like I was on a roller coaster, of sorts.This mother had been so close at times, just touching her to remember and believe she was home again, that Scotia felt like pushing her away but knowing that would cause more problems she just tried to play the part to the best of her ability.

"We have been mourning your loss for months now, My Dear Scotia, where have you been"?

Her new Mother grabbed for her hand and then laid her face on Scotia's cheek and cried. Trying to keep pace with this new story, Scotia, remembering things she had read in the tiny little book, replied that she had been kidnapped and that she had no idea that they were still alive, remembering what the diary had said, about the screaming and that she thought they were all killed. Her Mother hung her head and began to tell this overwhelming story from the Raid. hearing this whole story brought

Scotia to tears several times feeling the pity and the love they thought they had lost forever.

"A lot of the farm workers had been killed that day, and many of them had hidden and after the Vikings stole everything they could, the ship pulled off. We all came out of hiding and we tried to find you Scotia, but you were gone. The search went on for weeks. Everyone near and far from our home had heard about your disappearance and came to help us search.

We spent three days and nights in hiding,after they searched the Island for people hiding, and they quickly found more to kill, early one morning, as the winds whipped up the high waves,and the seas were calming down the vikings felt they that were calling to the Gods to go, and as soon as the sun was bright, very soon, the Viking men pulled the ship out to sea, we were so afraid Scotia, and then there had been no sign of you, and after the searching had finally been winding down, with no sign of any kind, not one man, woman, or servant had any news, because they had not seen you, you were and had been the topic of each conversation and each person on the island was beginning to grow weak with the fear that they had taken you.

The words kept singing in my mind and heart that I knew you could do it if it was possible. I knew you were so strong, and smart in hiding, and so we went on looking until there was no hope left at all, there were no signs anywhere that were visible.

And of all the people questioned no one had seen anything, being in hiding trying to save their own lives from these horrible killers, and so, it appeared all concerned thought they had killed you "

Holding onto what had to be her Mother from now on, with tears on every face in the crowd, Scotia felt all her fear of what she had been through, leaving her body as she felt the love of this different family surrounding her, and the ground under her feet felt so welcoming. Then she felt herself falling, someone got there and bax held her up, getting her mind clear, she knew was now in safe hands, feeling as good as she could she tried to smile. But she was not ready yet to think beyond today. All she could think at the moment was she didn't have to worry for a time now, and she would accept them as they accepted her. No more worries for a while thank God. Thank you God, now I have been rescued, her thoughts would be relaxed for a bit now. She felt a tenderness from this woman that she really needed. Of course she would not be her mother.

But still somehow, her mind knew they felt like the wrong family, and it was her saving grace, that she had them in this terrible situation at all, and of being lost it was for sure, extraordinary beginnings for her and so she went with the plan.

They began heading to the house in the distance, Scotia was following them, arm in arm with these people who she was told were her family.

Through this whole ordeal she had frightening flashes of other people and other times, and often a person called Elaine was there in her mind.

Her life had begun to take on a new aspect with these flashes and spending lots of time trying to understand these strange memories she was not able to really deal with yet, but she had no other plan and she was going to do this day by day.

And now these people were calling her daughter. From out of nowhere and from the Viking ship capture, this was a miracle. It felt like she knew them but at this point she felt like she would bond with anyone, but she also knew this was all new and felt a little bit safer with these strangers

Her situation before was feeling lost, but, then out of the blue she reached for the man's hand and began walking toward what these people called her home. Knowing that she most certainly had no idea where or who really was right at this moment.

She kept walking towards an unknown future. How this could be, her mind suddenly cleared up and she had a lot to deal with, but what she had before her now was wonderful, and comparing it to the boat it was a miracle.

At the same time, and remembering the ship and being so hungry and scared, and hiding for weeks, she felt a bit of happiness returning although with many reservations. And different kinds of worries. Also she was feeling very remorseful about the way she had handled her return with these people who were so concerned about their daughter. Knowing she was not the daughter and behaving as if she was, really did not make her feel too much better. She was determined to figure this out and she was going to start right now. For right now she felt landed and after what she had already been through, this by far was the best situation.

CHAPTER 17

After rummaging around her so-called room, and looking in all the drawers that she could pull open, was hard, with no pull knobs, and no handles, it all felt so awkward, but there were many signs, a girl had been here.

Something caught my eye on the wall. I saw hand drawn art. It was like a child's drawing but still had character and it surprised me that there were clearly lines here from an artist, not the girl who they thought I was, but their daughter. That's another story.

And the evening came, and they made me feel so loved. We shared a supper, also very different for me, then at first we had casual conversation, with non stop questions, which I did my best to answer, from each and everyone around this long table. I felt the need to make them understand. But the real truth was absolutely impossible to explain in any way at all.

The meal was so different from what I was used to, both from my home and from the ship, so I was now trying to eat more strange dishes again. Because I did not want to ever feel the starvation I had felt several times on that boat, there had been times when on the ship we ate whatever the cook found in his cooking area, and if they caught fish I got one bite, or some kind of old dried bread.

Most times it was some kind of strange looking meat. And trust me this was so strange to me, because I had never ever been hungry before.

I remember thinking, on the ship. Am I ever going to get a hamburger again? I sat and looked at the meals that they served on the ship. Day after day the same food. Not a single thing, even a potato, did I recognise.at first I thought about the food at home and so plentiful and I really felt so depressed that food after a while did not even enter my foggy brain. The days seemed to pass all the same.

Their drink was always alcoholic. No milk and no sweet tea. Oh how I had longed for the sweet tea my mother used to make every night at home. I longed for home.

Most of the men (if you could call them men) looked like the walking dead to me. This was when I took all precautions and hid, but I never knew when they slept. It seemed like I could see them walking all over the ship at all times of the day and night. These men would paint their faces in horrible colors, and they looked like the Indians from the reservations.

Something else I also worried about, was a bathroom at times, but there were times when they would all sleep with the command that I could hear, "keep watch from the timbers", I realized that was high up in the top sails of this ship, and no one would be looking for a tine girl sneaking around trying to find a crumb of anything to eat, or go to the bathroom.which was what did.

That was then and now I'm here with different days of my life that are constantly changing. I was not mistreated but I was ignored, no one cared enough to throw me a bone. But after the drunks passed out I would sneak out and find myself some old bread or something. That was then and now is different.

As I was laying in this bed of sorts I was thinking about how much more I could take, before I just cried.

When all of a sudden the door burst open and an old old man came rushing to my side and fell onto my bedside, trying to not cry. I was shocked and a bit frightened, to say the least then I said "please"as I pushed him to a sitting position. Once again I knew I had to put on my best smile and ask the right questions, and then lastly I had to make the story I had told these people come alive one more time, so I tried to hug him and then Pushed him back so I could stand up.

He had crocodile tears in his blue eyes. So I simply said "I think I know you "and he said yes and yes because I

Am your grandfather!`` His questions went straight to my heart, I felt his love as surely as I felt the sun on a bright warm morning, as surely as if he was my grandfather, and yet as my brain was rejecting this information, my heart felt his words and his love.

It was then that I began to put these pieces together, and I knew they truly had a daughter and granddaughter but obviously something had happened to her.

It was not my way of thinking logically, but the pieces did fit together with every new conversation I was having. The pieces fell together at last.

So was this my new life? Soon my Grandfather, patted my hands and said goodnight, and as he was reaching for the bolt on the door that should have been a door knob, I said "bye and I did miss you so much" he turned and the tears were back. Telling myself to 'shut up' I layed back down and prayed for my real life to come back and said my prayer that I had been saying for a while now, Dear God "Please let me wake up at home" I fell asleep. The last thing I was thinking was please God, as soon as possible take me home.

Morning came with the smells of food. As I turned over in this strange feeling bed, it was then the memories began to stir, and I remembered where I was. Throwing back those warm covers, that had felt like my sanest moment, in so long, I jumped up and with the thought of food that really did smell like bacon this time, I headed into the next room, and because I did not remember the layout from the night before, I went to where I heard many voices and also my hunger for the food was pulling me there, mostly the smell of bacon..

Opening the door quietly so I could see the layout of the room again, this time with a clearer mind, I wanted to take a seat by these people who thought I was their daughter. As hungry as I was it didn't matter at all that they were really strangers. Having experienced deja vu I had had many other similar occasions of deja in my life like this before, brought a memory of once I woke up screaming in my bed and my Mother had comforted me back to sleep. But in the morning I had no memory of the night before. So it had been lost to me.

As I sat there the thought in my mind this morning, sitting around, with all these people, my mind said, how can I ask what year it was, so as not to make them think I was not smart.

"Good morning"I said as I entered the small room where I could hear and see people and smell food. Food was the most important thing right at this moment to me. All eyes turned to me as I entered the small room with six other people sitting around a square wooden rough looking table that had food on it. I silently said a short prayer for the food. Then added a short thought saying silently "Please dear lord let them have bacon, and let them like me, until I can find my way back home. I hid the smile but I guess they were so happy to see me that they felt the same way. I asked when I had taken the rough old cracked wooden chair that I felt was going to break into at the moment, ``can I smell bacon?"

Saying the word home made me so sad and trying to imagine Elaine back there, all alone, and trying to untangle the fact that I was gone. And where was I, a thought I figured I might as well forget. This situation began when I picked up the little book in the very bottom of the old clock that had me in its grips now, and I was still processing this thought I guess.

Am I Scotia? But I knew better, and trying to make them understand was beyond me at this time.

Not a very good thought, So I stepped up and they all moved at once to make an open place for another chair. The food smell was everywhere. It looked like lunch to me, but at this moment food was food and I needed it to allow myself to get through this day ahead. I could only imagine all the questions I would be asked and my brain needed food to help me with, how to answer them, making it seem honest was not going to be easy at all, I said silently to myself "you can do it, you have no choice. So I sat down on the tiny chair they had provided for me in a very small place, because there were eight people there waiting with a barrage of questions that had no answers.

Ultimately I had always been a fast talker so I was prepared to spin a tale to make me dear to their hearts. I had picked up a lot of information from the day before so I had to play as if I was very confused, and anyway their expectations would have to wait until I had food in my stomach, then I would be able to figure out a simple story of tragedy. I was going to ask more questions and then, spin my story around the answers they were going to give me unknowingly.

Throwing it out as if I knew what I was talking about. One man asked me what bacon was, so I assumed I had spoken it out loud, even though I did not know it.

Completely confident that food would feed my brain I picked up my plate which I noticed at once was a rough hand made wood, rough like something you would feed your dog or cat out of, so I hid my surprise and tried to pick up the conversation that I had in mind when I said bacon."Oh"my brain said but I said, to my brain, it's like I have moved to a new house and all I have to do is find and remember my place, and it was going to be a normal conversation with all my fears and doubts gone! I was sure I could do it but first food was my ultimate goal.

After I sat down I looked at all these people and tried to decide which one I wanted to speak to first, that was if no one spoke to me after a few minutes. So I said, ``Did I smell bacon this morning?"no one answered, and again I said I thought I could tell what you were cooking, and I was hoping it was my favorite. I saw a few eyes raise then the lady who was my grandmother said "were you wanting your favorite meat Scotia?"I just smiled hoping she would say what it was so I could answer.

Searching the eyes of these eight people, I saw a lot of questions coming, and yet not one person had said a word first. So I thought it was time for me to start the morning off good, with a conversation that essentially I was hoping would help all of us.

"Good morning and first I want to thank you so much for the room and bed. It feels like I have not been in a good bed in a very long time, and last night I was so comfortable, "looking at the eyes I saw a lot of looks. So look, " if you would like we can discuss any questions you want to ask me because as I know you must have plenty, and must still be so worried about what has happened to me."

A smiling lady spoke up saying, "We want to make sure you try to remember us and your life before this thing happened to you, and we know it will all become clearer after a few good nights of sleep and some home cooking lessons. But we all noticed that you were not sure of our names and not sure what part we play in your life Scotia, and before the Viking raid, and this happened we had been cooking together, and you had accomplished a few new dishes and you had prepared them for us, which we had all really enjoyed."

Seeing the confusion in the lady's eyes, it suddenly came to me that it might be more than I could pull off.

So I began to tell them about "my memory and that there was not much I could say yet, because the bad memories were blotting out the good ones right now, but if you can give me time, I promise I will answer these questions", as long as they gave me time to come up with an answer

"I am still having fearful thoughts and thinking I can hear them coming after me".

Even as I slept I tossed and turned all night and the little sleep I did get was so just perfect for my first night back with these people, even though I have no idea who they are yet. Laughing to myself I began to dig, making up this story, about who I was and where I had been and when did I go? Oh there were so many faces waiting to hear it.

So there were many questions and answers that needed answers and I felt content and I knew that I could make them up if necessary and if not a lie would also work.

"Ok" I calmly questioned them, ``can you please tell me what you thought happened to me from the beginning". When did I disappear from here?"

I instantly saw the strange looks they shared. I figured I had said something wrong but with the looks on their faces, I could tell they were trying so hard to help me tell them what they needed to hear, so that it made me all confused all over again, and I needed time so I said please be patient, and I will be able to answer your questions, but it all feels so far away in my mind and the pictures are jumbled up good with bad and im in one place then another, but most of my memories are when I was hiding in the huge Grandfather Clock they had on board the ship. I saw looks pass through all their faces, and I wanted to explain but I knew it would just be more confusing and better all the way around if I could just eat something first so I said with fake tears in my eyes "please can I have some food first" and all at once everyone was handing my a different plate. So I made the decision to go with whatever it felt to me, like they could understand. I was hoping this would give me the answers for all the questions I knew were on their minds, and on the tip of their tongue right now...

About ten minutes had passed and the younger woman said "please may I interrupt you with a question we all have on our minds now about the Great big clock?"

I tried to smile but then I thought I had better play it up big time and maybe I could waste some time eating before I began the tale that I was conjuring up in my mind. It seemed it was going to be able to use this clock story and the little book that had apparently belonged to their daughter Scotia after all.

I tried to relax and when the breakfast was put down in front of me, I would take a small bite then tell something else I had just thought of to appease them and then I took it from there, saying how bad the food had been on that ship, and meat was not on that ship after the first three days went by. Then we had bread that some man would bake in the night because I could smell it, and it reminded me of here and your bread Mother." Seeing her smile I knew I had hit that right, and I told them that I had to go days with only water or milk, and it was warm milk, screwing up my face I noticed they were wanting to question me, so I said "does anyone have any questions here because it looks like you want to ask me something"? So I said then, keeping the conversation going, about how terrible the cook had been. "and about hiding in the huge Grandfather Clock, to which I had started calling my Grandmother clock. With that said everyone began smiling and the conversation went with questions to me, about me and I felt the love all around me.

"Then what was wrong with the milk Scotia?' the mother said, I was disappointed that I had not gotten them off the subject of my comment about the warm milk.

So I added "did you not remember that I loved cold milk?" they all looked at me like I had grown three heads, and I saw them look towards the windows then back to each other with questions

Gazing off into the morning sunshine I began to worry if I would ever be me again, and would I stop time traveling, because, that's what I was thinking now for a while, was going on, because how could I keep being someone else.

And I thanked God that I could remember things that were becoming important to me as every day went by or always someone else, and where would all this lead me in the end, I guess I was supposing there was an end somewhere out there. I would have to pretend to be. Now back to my breakfast that looked different but I didn't care because it looked delicious to me.

Taking it from there I took my fork, and got a big plate of some kind of meat, stringy with fatty gristle on the underside, when I was trying to cut it up.

It was mixed with eggs and gritty tasting flour, maybe. Also they had put a bowl of porridge in front of me. It did not matter what it was right then because I was too hungry, and so I ate every bite.

In between mouthfuls of strange foods, I was able to explain the simplest things that then had these people asking many more questions. So with my imagination

I made the adjustment to be who they wanted me to be, and saw the people relaxing, and all of a sudden I felt their love in the room, for a stranger they thought was their sister.

Later after the question and answer game I asked to be able to take a nap and then told them after I got up, I wanted to talk to everyone else who was there, so looking around and seeing new faces, I knew I needed to learn these names and faces, as quickly as my mind would allow. I felt alone, trying to remember, but they spent their time trying to remind me of things, and asking me things that the real Scotia knew. I felt trapped by these people and at the same time I saw love shining in their eyes for the sister they thought I was.

I smiled at them as I walked to my room. And then I made myself calm down. Closing my eyes I immediately fell asleep.

Somewhere in my dream there was a person I had called Elaine. She had called me sister several times. We Seemed to be very close, the conversation I could remember from my fast deleting memories, was about somewhere and antiques. And we also were talking about a long and tiring plane ride. But even though I felt like I should get the conversation, I still was not too sure.

Laying there on the soft bed, which I noticed was strange because it had no springs or even a frame, I rolled over and closed my mind to these new uncomfortable intrusions, and names. But somehow I felt it was very important to remember the name Elaine. I stored it with all the other memories for right now.

CHAPTER 18

Somewhere in the back of my mind I had visions of a Great Big Suit Of Honor. My mind recoiled to this information. So closing my eyes was the thing I was sure would help me in the long run to get back to wherever I was supposed to be.

Laying there I dozed again, and this time my memories prevailed.

I saw Elaine, we were in a dark and gloomy room, all around us were the two things we were searching for, and when the connection clicked, I was not sure where I was, but when Elaine touched my arm and told me, "there is an old building over there"and pointed left, I suddenly saw other things.

Later, I was to understand these things that were flying through my mind, would have to be overlooked while I made a new approach to where I was now...But where was I right now, and who was Scotia, and what about the clock, the great big Grandfather Clock,what did it mean? And how did I get on that ship with murderers?

And what year could this be? Nothing made any sense or had any correlation to me now.

I really needed to know the year for my mind set. I had to believe I would be able to find my way home again, to my best friend and sister who I had talked into coming to antiquing so soon after our las

It seems that everyone else knew, but I did not actually remember anything before these people came and called me Scotia. Suddenly it occurred it was me who they were calling Scotia, but I did remember my name, I was Glenda. The dream was helping, and how convenient to know who I was now. But how did I end up here? There must be answers somewhere, and I was going to find them come Hell or High waters. ThenI was thinking to myself where did that phrase come from?

It must have been a couple hours later that I heard someone in the room. Turning over to see who it was I saw the man who had been calling me his granddaughter. He was walking easy as if not to wake me. I suddenly sat up to see better. He was about to leave when I called out to himnot to leave. Turning around with a great big smile on his face I almost wished he was my Grandfather. He walked back to where I was sitting up in this bed.

"Honey, he said, with the most heart warming tone to his voice,I'm so happy to see you looking rested"

It seemed that I remembered someone calling me honey before.but that was all I could remember. Looking back at the man I said, thanks very much "Thanks so much Sir."

There were a lot of his questions I could not answer with a clear mind, so I just smiled a lot,since I had accepted all these people into my new world it was going to be touch and go until I got my memories back.

Almost ready to answer him about how I had just wanted a little nap, I spoke up. "Yes, I am still trying to remember how I ended up on that ship."

He just smiled and said "I'm sure it will all come back in time, so don't fret over these memories that are not clear yet."

I had a lot of memories but none of them were clear at all yet. Feeling like in time they would be clear was how I put on my smile and walked into the other room to learn whatever I could. I listened carefully but no information hit me, as I had hoped I would learn some more.

His smile was so warming that I felt at ease instantly. Sitting up I swung my legs over the edge of this bed and began to slide to the floor. I noticed the black floorboards. They had to have been cut from a tree one by one, I just knew it. My mind was blown away trying to imagine the amount of hard work that entailed. I did not see any cut marks or saw holes, or not even one nail.

So I decided to follow my nose and entered the main room where all the conversation was coming from. Each person had a look that said let me talk first. I almost laughed and instead I went to pull out one of the chairs around the beautiful, large table.

"Im so much better now with the rest"I said to answer all the looks coming my way.

The rest of the afternoon and into the dinner hour we talked and I tried to learn what I needed to know about this situation. I did not learn anything new, and decided after about two hours of each one of them firing questions at me that I needed to give up. Because there was nothing that even sounded like it made sense. It was all aboutScotia. We were talking and I was answering questions as fast as they came at me. It was funny in a way. But the hours went by fast. From everything I had heard there this afternoon, nothing made any sense so I spoke up and said "please let me tell you what I remember and then we can go from there,ok?"

Smiles came all around the table and so I started feeling a confidence I really didn't have.

Speaking up and seeing all eyes on me I said, "I know you are waiting for something I can't really give you, but here is what I do remember, and it is not really going to make sense so please remember that I can not remember everything all at once, but I'm going to try, to make you understand if you can. So Please Listen With ears and your mind."

"This won't make you understand what I'll say,but it is all I have right now, is this going to be ok with you all?" Looking around the table, I was waiting for someone to answer or nod, maybe yes or no, and I saw looks and questions, but not really any answers from any one of the people sitting there in that cozy little room they call a kitchen.

I said and cleared my throat my first ideas of how to let this information sink in just one brain and from there I knew they would share their thoughts and then I might get lucky and see them believe.

"Ok so here goes" please listen carefully, and I saw them glance at each other like I spoke French, "this is why I do not know where I am and I promise I am not Scotia and I do not know Scotia."

She saw some questions coming but avoided them by speaking up first, saying, "first of all my name is not scotia, and I see the looks in all your eyes but wait and listen to me first please ok?"A few heads nodded yes, so she set off again,"Here is what I know, my name really is Glenda, and when I woke up in that horrible, rocking, stinking ship and I was hiding in the bottom case of a huge Grandfather Clock. I see your questions, but hold on. I think I was hiding in the clock case from those

Vikings trying to stay alive. But even before that, I have a huge memory loss."I could see the word memory caused a little stir, but they were hearing me.

I promise I will try my best to help us all understand by telling the bits and pieces I can remember, do you think you can hear me and try to understand? Because why would I tell you these things if they were not true?.

There was some movement and I saw them all looking back and forth from one face to another "

I saw doubt and disbelief but in a few faces I saw hope.

"By the way would you mind telling me the date today?". As I saw a few heads turn, I picked up the conversation again, because I could see the doubt on their faces, and so holding onto my positive attitude I spoke up quickly to hide the doubt that I might be an idiot. "My mind is so confused but everything I see so far is not like my home. "They all shared looks of dismay. And I could almost read their faces. They were saying "poor Scotia, Oh my word what is wrong with our child?"

Finally one of them looked directly at me and said ``Scotia the year is 1438 and we are in Constantinople, the month is May and the day is the 7th."

They were all sharing looks, back and forth they went until I stood up and said,"let me explain please. "So first of all you have no idea what it is like to be trapped in the bottom of a grandfather clock for days, and the weather was so hot, and I was so hungry that I heard myself crying one evening and I was so scared that someone had heard me that I felt the need to hide for longer periods of time after that night.

One man just had to ask me how did I fit inside this clock? So I promised if he would let me finish I would answer his question.

"I remember seeing it on the ship and the first evening I crawled up to it and pulled the glass door open and when I saw how large the clock was I climbed right in and got down really low so no one would ever see me in there. I had been put on the bottom deck, after the raid and after they forgot about me I snooped around at night when they were all drunk and crazy. There were other women on the boat so no one even remembered the little girl they had stowed on board that night after they had fought all the pirates off.

After I got my sea legs and could finally eat I had to crawl out in the night after they all passed out and fell everywhere from the drinking, and found scrapes that barely kept me alive. But, alive I am and now I do not want to let you down but trust me I'm not Scotia!

"I promise you my name is Glenda!"

With that said, the strange looks went from one face to the next face and soon. I didn't know what they were going to think or believe, but I saw a look in the lady's face. I think she was their fierce leader through all things good and bad.

'How did these VIkings find you?' was the next question. And it was then that I heard a voice in my ear, "make up something, anything and make it sound good. Do you hear me?

I felt as if it was Elaine telling me with her mind even though she had no idea where I might be. We had a very close relationship, and I felt her pulling for me.I knew if she had been there with

Well the point was, I did not know and was also battling my own demons at the time.

So I started with the truth, slowly looking from face to face I began to tell my story, "I am from another time also…watching all the faces staring at me. I was so surprised that not one of them had opened their mouth or even looked dumbfounded at my statement.

Worrying that they would give up on my story, which I knew would be so hard for them to believe, I said "please give me time", I asked "please do not give up on me because everything I said is the God's truth. Just give me time and then think, ``Why would I try to make up stories if I am really your daughter?" seeing looks go from person to person, the man spoke up and said, "we will listen but do you not know who you really are? Because we do know who you are.

"I respect that you must think I'm absolutely certified crazy."She saw them looking from one to the other, knowing they were having a hard time believing her. Especially my new words. By now she was crying to them, I wish I was her but….

"I really want to be your Scotia but the truth is I'm not".

Tears were falling from the face of the Grandmother and the others were looking at each other trying to find a way to believe her. She knew she looked like her, and they were trying hard to listen, but they just couldn't do it, not yet anyway."

This was so stressful, looking from face to face and seeing disbelief and some tears from the ladies, I tried again.

"I know, but would you want me to lead you on and let you believe I'm her then one day poof I disappear?" Because, trust me, poof and I was here!!"explaining she said POOF is a magical word for something that appears from nowhere, then in a blink of an eye it was gone as fast as it showed up. Explaining, she saw them smile a tiny bit. But she didn't think they really got it at all.

She saw the looks on their faces. Taking up her speech again she said, "Do you remember how I turned up here?"

She could tell the word poof did not go over too well. She had tried to explain the word but even then she saw disbelief in their eyes, and she knew the next thing that they would have to believe was that her mind was gone and they would offer all their help to her recover from the disaster on the Viking ship She had to make a decision and she needed to reassure them that until she could return to her time she would be whoever they needed her to be. It really was so sad that she looked like the missing girl Scotia.

Seeing and hearing so much disbelief she decided to ask for some time. "Ok" looking at them she told them she needed to rest and then she would tell them everything she remembered and answer all their questions. One lady said "poof and you will be gone? She turned to look at the other 8 people sitting there for approval that they could try to believe her. "I don't want you to worry, here is what I'm hoping will happen, if I stay here maybe in a little time the real Scotia might show up and the end of this mystery might turn out to end well."

I'm going to have a rest then I hope you make a scrumptious dinner".

Looking at the one who had been cooking, she threw her a kiss, to their amazement, because she saw the look in their eyes. Turning around to go to the room they called hers, she felt a breath of fresh air but this was only round three, and she fell asleep, trying to decide what the next move would be and if they were going to believe her at all.

CHAPTER 19

Later that evening, after the really first good sleep since she had turned up there, with her mind made up she walked back into the kitchen ready to try some more explaining.

Everyone was still sitting in the same chairs at the table, she smiled a big smile and took a seat at the table. Making conversion she tried to watch the faces looking for some reaction to her appearance and her story.

They were all smiles so she began again, "there is something I forgot to try to explain last night.

I want to tell you a story about me and where I really come from. If you will listen searching their faces for a certain look I wanted I saw it was not there yet, so smiled at each one and said "let me try again to explain my life before I ended up on that viking ship filled with cold calculated murderers.

"OK, here goes, Do you remember what I told you about having a sister? No one moved, so I went on, "I have a sister, "watching their faces for evidence that they heard me and maybe they could believe this story, I saw nothing at all in the way of an expression or belief that they told me they believed me.

I went on, "Her name is Elaine and we would always travel together from our home to London England in search of two particular old antiques. "

There was not a shadow of recognition in these faces of what I had told them before, because I realized they probably hadn't listened when we first met and when I told them I was not Scotia it did not register at all.

Hoping to get part of this done and a few more faces smiling I started to talk again....

"Ok try to imagine two sisters in an old antique store," in a different country, when one of us goes missing. That someone was me. Are you still with me?" I looked all around the room and saw not one face with even a tiny bit of understanding on them.

I turned around and went to a small window in this tiny room, wondering how I was going to get through this. Looking out at the dark bleak night I really was worried about what was going to happen next, It was getting dark outside and the ladies went about lighting some of the tiny lights all around the kitchen. I sat there waiting and hoping that someone would have a question but no one said a word.

Then out of the blue one boy sitting there all quiet and solemn said "maybe if she was our Scotia she would have made us aware of some of the things she knows that we also know".

Everyone looked at him and I saw them nodding their heads. I felt a jolt of excitement in the fact that even if only one might believe, that later on they all would begin to believe.

So while they were cooking or whatever you could call what they were doing, it started to smell good. Of course I was so starved and had been hungry ever since they found me that this smell made me smile.

It had only been three days since they found me but I was beginning to feel comfortable here. It was definitely more comfortable than the Grandfather Clock had been. And at least I did have a room that they called my own.

The meals were beginning to look appetizing even though I felt simple minded having to ask what was this and what is that? The cook would look at all the other faces to see if I was the only one who did not like to hear her ask questions about every bite that she put in her mouth. As days went by I noticed that I was becoming overjoyed with the megar food. Tonight I decided not to ask about anything and just enjoy this part of whatever was going on, and with these kind people I had to make it simple from now on.

Mallie, who was supposed to be my Mother, asked me to tell her a story after dinner.

I imagined that she wanted to try to open up my mind and see what I did know and then she could put a name on me.

In between bites of whatever this was on my plates,

I said, "What did your Scotia call you?" Everyone was in between bites and it felt like time was standing still. I only waited a few seconds and then I said "Please don't worry, but what did she call you? I really need to know."

There were tears in her eyes. I stood up and went to her and put my arms around her and felt her sobbing. "Please don't cry. I promise we will all adjust to my lack of knowledge in time. And I have a great hope in my heart that your Scotia will show up soon and we can all understand how time has misplaced me."

Well, looking around at all the faces I saw not one bit of hope in anyone's eyes but mine.

I didn't want to cause more trouble so hoping it would turn the conversation away from me and my words, I asked what kind of meat we were eating"?

It only got more weird looks from at least three of them. But my Mother did know supposedly it was my favorite. That left me with nothing else to say. So I started to yawn as if I was so tired. Saying goodnight and hugging my Mother I said "see you in the morning."

Laying in this so not comfortable bed I knew I wasn't mentally strong right now. Turning over to try to think I went immediately to sleep. Sometime in the night I had to use the bathroom, but oh no I needed the strength to go outside to relieve myself.

Trying to be quiet I finished and then headed toward the front of the house, when I saw something coming through the field.

Just a shadow at first but then it took shape and kept moving straight to this house. I tried to make myself invisible and never made a move. I didn't have the ability to stand still for long so I just sat down on the step and watched. As the person got closer they started to run, awkwardly like a girl. As if she knew where she was going, maybe like her home? I wondered to myself who or whom it could be in the middle of the night

Thinking about it and trying to slowly stand up and not frighten her I waved my hand. To maybe warn whoever it was that she was being watched by someone… Even though it was not morning yet, I knew the person saw me. I felt the distinct knowledge that whoever this was, was heading straight to her home. At first the closer she got to me she saw me, and then slowed down.

Now since I was the problem solver here at this moment I decided to wave. Putting my hand in the air I waved.

The person waved back but not with the certain knowledge that she knew who I was. It felt like she slowed down and was taking even longer to get closer here. Then she was there and staring at me. Who she was I did not know but she looked a lot like me. It was a few minutes and it came to me that this must be the real Scotia. All at once I just sat down and waited for the questions I knew were coming. She stood there, and she looked like me, and I did look like her.I could see the questions in her mind. My brain was screaming "this is the real Scotia"so I reached out my hand and she took it. I felt the hands tingle. I knew this was my salvation, but in the other way I had nowhere to go so I wondered if these people would let me stay, if this was the real Scotia, until I found a way to go home again.

She looked in my eyes and then she said "you look like me? "Yes I know and your Mother doesn't understand this at all. She thinks I am you, so now I'm so happy, because you are safe and back home. Let me go wake her and try to make this easy for all three of us, ok?" She smiled and I saw a real resemblance to myself. Inside my brain was thinking of all the things that might happen when they realized I was not their Scotia. My brain was overreacting to this. Oh God what will happen now?

This little girl took my hand and we walked inside to people who were waking up and walking into the warmest part of the home, the kitchen, to start another day.

The first person to see her standing there by me was her Mother. She blinked her eyes and then she started to cry loudly enough for the rest of the people to wake up and run to her so scared there was something that had happened.

Seeing her daughter standing there next to me she rubbed her eyes and started to rush to her. After a hug and warm welcome the mother turned to stare at me, pushing her daughter behind her, and then turned to her daughter for confirmation that this was truly her daughter.

The whole day went by in a blur with the heart felt homecoming and the loving family coming together again, taking time for questions, and answers.

It seemed that she had been captured by the Vikings and was held in ropes for the whole time. She had burns on both wrists and deep gashes in a bloody streak down the right side of her back.her ribs were almost pushing out of her tight skin from starvation on the Viking ship.

She had been treated as I had but I wondered where she had been taken compared to where I had been. Thinking back I remembered that there were three tall ships all with black flags the same as the one I was held in, so she must have been captured too that same day.

Immediately I spoke up because I wantedto say that I was so sorry they had not believed me, and how happy I had been to have been treated so kindly by strangers, smiling as if to say, that even if I did look like their daughter,how happy I was that she was home safe with her family again.

It gave me a reason to live again, but I had no idea how to ever get back where I wanted to be. I really knew I had to stay there until whatever had happened to me that landed me there would go away.

It felt very different from then on and I tried to imagine what would happen to me now, with the real Scotia returning to her home. How or when I would go back in real time and home, or if I ever would. But seeing that she had come back home I had hopes that I would go back to my sister too.this scene before me brought tears and wracking sobs from me that I had no control over at all.

It was taking a long time to focus on this new situation. As the sun came up this morning, the food and conversation took over everything that had been a normal habit here at this time, in yesterday's time

I had to be prepared as much as possible to begin to become who I really was, Glenda. A person from another time in a world where no one would ever believe me.

Just to say my name to myself, I made a glowing smile cover my face, and my heart was beating really fast and hard with the new situation,I watched all the faces of the people who truly had begun to believe I was Scotia, and they were definitely confused.

I drank my milk and my mind was working overtime. What would they think now, if I said they would let me stay here until I found a way back to my time? I really thought that because of the time I had spent there that they all had some kind of feelings for me, and that comforted me greatly...

"Everyone please gather in the eating room now so we can all gather and ask all the questions we need answers for. And because our Scotia has returned all safe and not harmed in any way it looks like we are truly blessed to have two Scotia's".

The rest of that day went by slowly with everyone there asking so many questions and the answers were not easy to hear. The torture the real Scotia indurred was unimaginable as when compared to mine capture. By dinner time I had come up with a new idea, I wanted to ask my new step mother if I could call her by the name the rest of the family called her "Mallie"? She finally let go of the real Scotia, giving her a kiss and push to the soft fur covered chair that she said was Scotia's favorite chair since her father had killed this huge bear when she was four years old, and made this chair especially for her.

Turning to me she took me in her arms and held me fast until she took me to the chair at the dinner table that I had been sitting in since my arrival here and sat me down and then took a chair next to me. I felt really insecure right then. My mind kept going to the inevitable, maybe being turned out and on my own again.

Where would I go if they turned me out now that they had their Scotia back in their midst.

My stomach was in turmoil, my nerves were pulsing through my mind. I was so very frightened about the outlook of my future and where would I go and how would I survive, so I kept a low profile and said nothing, just smiling and wringing my hands while I thought my future might be taking a turn for the worse.

After the homecoming and all her family reuniting with their lost child, everything went back to the normal that I had learned in my time being there.

The Grandfather took my hand and said that he understood how she had been lost and that the VIkings had taken her but he also told her as he squeezed her tiny hands that she was not going anywhere because they had all begun to love her with the love they had for the real Scotia. Then he took a seat by bringing them both chairs to sit in.

He said she had been a very special gift that the Gods had sent to them while their Scotia had been stolen from them. Through the weeks she had been there they had formed a bond that they could not ever refuse.

That the whole family really loved her,as she was and not as their Scotia, but the new Scotia, just Scotia who had become their daughter too. He told her her life would be there as usual, just being herself. The feeling that went over her was unexplainable, it was a warmth and love that she had grown accustomed to since she walked over that hill and they had first seen her, all alone and surely as lost as anyone could have been in her situation.

The whole family had accepted her and wanted her to keep her there with them until and if something turned around she went home again. He also asked her to tell them how this had affected her life since being captured. And that the real Scotia and herself would share the sleeping room together as it had always been their Scotias.

He told her he had high hopes that together they can heal from this horrible thing that had happened to them both. The fact that they had both been through such an experience it made them the perfect roommates. He waited for her to speak but she had only tears to shed at first. This meant something bigger and different to her, as much as she had become a part of their family she still had homesickness and melancholy for quite a lot of her time there. With this plan in her hands she turned towards the real Scotia and then asked them if she could be called Glenda from then on."it makes sense that your kindness for me would be better spent calling me my real name since the real Scotia was in the home now once again safe and sound. They all smiled and she became Glenda that night...

That night in her bed with Scotia they hugged and talked throughout the night comparing their situations each to the other. It felt like to Glenda that they both had been spared by something equally magical and by the only God Glenda really knew. The rest of these people had never talked about worship to her or in her presence before and so she had kept quiet throughout all of this ordeal.

CHAPTER 20

First thing in the morning they ate the unusual food they called breakfast. Then Mallie sent them to the creek to do some washing up with the biggest basket of dirty clothes she had ever imagined in all her life. The noon sun was so hot shining down on them and the cool breezes were blowing their hair out of their faces which helped a lot because as they swished the clothes in and out of the water, they kept cool. The soap she had anticipated was never brought up. A man did bring them what he called soap, but not in my mind had I ever seen such a big rough scratchy bar of soap!

Just a rough piece of wood that she watched her namesake rub the dirty clothes back and forth until they were called clean by her namesake. After a while She asked the real Scotia about how she hoped that the people would now call her by name. She told her about her sister and about her name Elaine, and that she really was Glends.

Who immediatley told her she had never heard a name like that before. Thinking it was too soon to mention how she ended up there and anything about her real home, she just smiled and they kept washing the huge heavy basket full of clothes that the two of two them could hardly handle alone.

Glenda, was deep in thought when the sun which was shining down so warmly on them bounced off of something shiny and she thought that she saw some kind of broken glass shining deep in the water as it swished over the big rocks and ran right toward them.

"Hey watch out so that you don't get cut because I saw some broken glass come running over those rocks headed right to where we are rubbing our clothes. Scotia spoke up and said it was not glass but some kind of rocks that she had seen many times when they were washing clothes.

My feeling like what if it was diamonds, she reached in and grabbed a couple of the shiny stones as the water swooshed by them. Stepping back she opened her hand to see what she had found. At first she thought she would faint. In her hands she was holding gold nuggets, and not small ones either. They were big as a dime. After the shock she ran down stream to show Scotia what she had found. Not impressed at all it made me realize that if I had found Diamonds they were just like rocks here. But somewhere in my mind I had already decided to take a few big chunks to my room with me for the ever present hope to return home to 2020 sooner than later, with a fortune that I was bringing back with me from my trip of another time. Lately it was the way I would think about my daily life here. And if those were gold I still wouldn't be able to prove where I found them or make anyone understand the things I had been going through

"Glenda," Scotia spoke up, "I also know where there are a lot more shiny and beautiful rocks, they are in the deep bottom of this pool that I know, way down there by the big stand of trees with fruit on them."

I was trying to see where she was pointing at a spot that almost and certainly was a grove of some kind of fruit trees not far "and the rocks are big shiny ones. Looking towards the area she was pointing at, I grew so curious.. The trees were not too far away so she said "when we're finished scrubbing away with these clothes, let me show you".

"It is the most cool and beautiful spot. It always makes me wish we had brought something to take and eat down there, and when we were small children we played with those beautiful rocks all the time as my mother did the washing up.

Looking over there at the spot I spoke up and told her "yes let's walk down there" my mind was going in a hundred different ways, mostly thinking that I couldn't wait to see what these shiny rocks looked like. "Scotia" I asked, "are the stones rock or are they clear and shiny?" She looked at me and said she remembered the one she brought to her room, because it was so beautiful, and now I wanted to know if she still had it in her room? Immediately my brain said to my mind let's find it, so I could see it of course, and I laughed at the thought that I might be talking to myself and it did not matter anymore because everyday there were new things for me to observe and learn to live with, so to me they had to be Diamonds.

Wow! was all I could think, and because at this time there was no way to spout off about Diamonds and their value, so I only talked about the beauty of them. What else could I do? We began to walk down stream and through a grove of trees that had a fruit on the branches, but I didn't remember ever seeing those before. I walked up close and pulled a piece of it off and tried to smell it for a clue as to what kind it was. But eventually I threw it down, not a bit wiser as to what it might be. Following Scotia we headed down to the creek.I was wiping the sweat off my brow as I followed her straight to the bit of water in front of us. We walked down the steep bank and I saw nothing but she pointed to the area where she said there were a lot of the stones. But she called them rocks. Stepping down into the water I was swishing my feet in the muddy bottom of the water, and I could feel rocks because they were hurting my feet. I bent over and sat down in the water. There were no stones here. "Let's go down there," Scotia said to me, pointing to the bend in the creek. ``That is where I found them the first time."We carried on a question and answer time and the more she talked the more I began to believe that I might be able to find these diamonds and or the gold she mentioned to me, but it wouldn't matter at all because in this time they meant nothing.

Although I was still praying every day that things would change, and I would get the chance to go home again, I was still so excited to reach the place she told me about. I couldn't believe that I would see real diamonds and or gold so plentiful that we could gather bags full.

It wouldn't do me any good but the thought of having it in my hands was something exciting to see.

And then I saw her wave her hand to me like here it is hurry up. I rushed and as soon as I got close to the water I saw the shiny gold things in the water. I looked at her and her smile was like 'ok I TOLD YOU SO" squatting down I reached into the water feeling the cold water rushing over my hand, and I picked up a handful of dirt but the gold rocks were really gold in the sense of thousands of dollars in my time. Looking towards Scotia I saw her pick up more and then in the midst of her gold find I saw what I felt to be diamonds. She walked over to me and put her hands out to give me some of what she had. I just fell down in the water from the shock. Only in a Jewelry Store had I ever seen such beautiful shiny diamonds. And the gold rocks were possibly worth a million dollars. Of course in my time only, but I could not even share what I knew because I wanted these people to be good to me. And they most certainly had been so far.

My mind was as excited as I had ever been in a very long time. I walked back to the grassy bank and sat down to think. "My goodness you look so happy" Scotia said as I sat down.

Looking towards her as I saw her with hands full of uncut diamonds my smile got bigger. I knew that she had no idea why I was smiling and so I just shook my head and agreed with her. Sitting down by me we poured the wet dirt on the ground in front of us. She had more pieces of gold than I did but when we put our hands in my dirt pile I saw I had more dirt and so I had more gold pieces in my lap. She had a lot of both diamonds and gold nuggets.

We talked a bit and then we laid back tolet the sunshine in, while she had no idea what was in front of us. I on the other hand knew exactly what we had. But there was no way to make her understand what the value of these stones could really be, in my time of course, but in her time there was no way she would be able to know. I had to ask her about gold.``while I was on the ship I saw metal bands on the pirates arms and in their ears and I remember once late at night I was hiding in the base of the clock and they were all drinking whiskey I guess, but they were so drunk and I heard them talking about jewels they had stolen and one or maybe more began talking about who they were going to give them to. So I imagine these are worth a lot of money."I saw her look like she had no idea what I was talking about or even if she knew the word money, so I changed my conversation. It was such a beautiful day with the warm sun and cloudless sky overhead that I decided to ask some questions and see what they did in this new time I was in, the time when or how they married. When I said the word married I saw a strange look on her face..I knew I was going in the wrong direction. "How would this look if I made a ring out of it for my finger". At first she said nothing. Then she asked me what the meaning of marriage was.

Then I knew it was called something else because I had been reading a novel a while ago and in Scotland they were handfasting each other, not getting married. So I knew I had to go back to my studies when I was younger and try to remember some details if I could manage.

Changing the subject I said "when people are living together at this time what do they call it? I saw her strange look.

"Like your mother and father for example, does she wear a wedding ring?

What do you call this relationship now? Still not understanding I went deeper, "so when your mother and father first met did they go to a church to be together?"

"They were betrothed and that's a seal for them."

Smiling, I thought about some questions for her, hoping she could answer, "do you know if your mom" and I saw a look on her face,so I said, "Mom is Mother just shortened for conversation, ok?" she responded with a smile and a shake of her head. My intent on this questioning was to learn of any jewelry they might have and she could describe it to me. feeling like I needed to change the subject I said "this gold color metal rock we have found is most certainly gold. In my home my mother wears a wedding ring that symbolizes that she and my Dad were married in the eyes of God."

Now there was another look on her face. "Who is this man called God?" at this I was lost. And then I changed the subject.

What I wanted to say I already knew she would not understand, so I said "Do you pray at night?" she shook her head like she had no idea what I was talking about. Then I said do you, or the family attend religious Churches? Then I thought about it and asked 'who did the ceremony when people died or got married or had a new baby to Baptize?"

The look was absolutely blank "Look I know when people die there has to be a ceremony at the burial right?"

still the blank look. "So when people get married, who does it?" Scotia didn't understand so I tried one more thing, "If I wanted to be married, who would Marry me to my new husband?"

I waited and then she twisted her fingers and hands and said some days there is a traveling group who come through and they do these marriages. But we do not know when so there are not any actual ceremonies like you talk about."

At once I remembered, things here are nothing like my life had been and as long as I was here I had to bend.

"Ok lets get our stash and take it home for them to google," then I laughed. And I saw in her eyes she was lost again and I had to get it together, asking her what I thought would be the answer to me, or saying things without thinking kept bringing me to a difficult place. So I tried again.

"Scotia, do you get annoyed with me when I keep saying things you do not understand"? I watched her face for a sign. Just a tiny smile I saw. Changing my tone and my questions, I smiled too.

"Ok, this is what I want to do, I want to come back tomorrow and get some of these pretty clear stones and bring them back to my room. "Ok?" looking at her I saw no real questions coming, but I already knew she thought they were rocks, so I offered my thoughts about why I want the stones.

"Those stones are so beautiful, and I want to keep some for my collection"

Looking at her eyes I saw a collection was not something she knew of either, so I smiled and started to pick up a few to carry home with us.

Walking and talking I tried to tell her what the collection was."I collect things to make me happy. Like these rocks and their beauty make me smile.

My mind was thinking of a way to display them in the home that would make them think I had an original idea and they might even like it and want to get more...

"So we can come back whenever you want to, but I think the gold rocks are more beautiful and I'll collect some of them for me", smiling. I saw her begin to move towards the other part of the stream Following behind her, with my hands full of diamonds I could not help but think what people at home would say if they ever had a chance to see this.It was hard to even imagine.that I was going back home let alone bringing diamonds and real gold nuggets with me when and if I returned to my own time..

We were walking and I changed the subject so we had something to talk about together, and then she said to me "what did you mean that your family wouldn't believe you when they saw the gold?" and I answered, before thinking it out. Trying to come up with an answer that did not need more questions, I said that my friends and I loved shiny rocks and that now I was thinking about their faces when I showed them these so-called rocks that I knew for a fact was gold! Smiling, I kept the conversation going but tried to change the subject.

When a thought came to my mind, I asked her if the ladies ever wear jewelry, and did her mother wear a wedding ring. And then I was reminded that she didn't know what a wedding was, and the other conversation had been yesterday. Changing the subject so often these days kept me in a moment of always thinking before I spoke most of the time.

Looking up and seeing the sun going lower in the sky I said "we better get going" and I pointed to the sun. Walking slowly and carrying the Diamonds that I had to remember to call rocks, and the gold that I also had to name yellow stones, my mind was so full of things I needed to remember that I had started to not talk. Scotia looked at me and then I realized that she was waiting for an answer to something that I had not even heard her say.

I spoke up and asked her what she thought her mother was going to fix for dinner that night. Waiting for an answer I turned toward her face and said "Scotia did you hear me?" She was obviously thinking but not about her dinner meal.

When she looked up at me she had a look on her face that I had not seen before, "what is wrong Scotia?" "Well you know we do not ever know what our mom is fixing until we join her and sit down."

And I thought about what she said and remembered that we sat down to strange food every day. "Ok yes but my mother always had a list for us and we knew, and I'm hungry so I'm thinking about the surprises we might have tonight for our supper.. She was smiling now so I knew she understood what she meant…

Scotia said 'ok but you do know what we eat because you have been here a long time now". With a smile I shook my head yes and we kept walking. It did not take long I thought to get to her house, and before long these so-called rocks were getting heavier with each step, "Scotia tomorrow if we come back let's bring some kind of bucket with a handle to make it easier to carry to whatever we find or decide to bring back with us" she smiled and we walked on to the house I had begun to call home..

When we walked in the door, Scotia's Mom looked at us like we were in trouble and so I smiled and held out the bucket for her to see what we had been doing all afternoon. With the look on her face, of the Mom that had offered me a home, I felt like her daughter. Holding up the bucket with the large gold nuggets in it, she reached out her hand and said, "what have you girls been doing? Picking up rocks?" We both nodded our heads yes.

"Well I do think you have brought home some pretty rocks but whatever do you need with them?"

Scotia explained that we wanted to make a flower garden like I had told her about. Her Mom was looking at me like I had two heads. "Why would you want to use these ugly dirty rocks in a garden, and what is a garden anyway?" suddenly realising I did not know if they even had a garden I came up quick with a question to throw them off.

"I haven't seen any flowers or vegetables growing here but I had a thought that if you wanted me to show you how I had beautiful flowers in my garden at my home I would love to do it" she smiled at me as if to coddle a kid into believing she knew what I meant so I just smiled back. It actually seemed to work.

"Can we go outside and find a place for our rocks?" the mother with her hands on her hips nodded yes. And I also saw a smile there. I really did think she was beginning to think I was her daughter, which I really needed right now, in this place in my life I was getting used to things but I issued all my friends and my own Mother so bad.

"Look at your feet and you have mud and dirt all over you. So I think we better get this garden done so you two can clean up".

"And look at your feet" she exclaimed, her eyes wild and her expression was one I hadn't seen on her face before, like maybe angry?

I asked her to show us where it would be ok to make a garden, and I could see in her expression that she was getting aggravated slowly but surely. So I said ``can we do it in the corner here where not many people walk"? I saw her looking and then she nodded her head yes. We were so excited.

"Do you have a hoe"? They both looked at me like I was crazy so I changed the wording some to make them understand what I was needing. I walked over to the corner of the grass where I thought it would be perfect to place the gold rocks (My Gold) in a triangle shape for the time being. Sitting on the ground I moved about and placed the border of my garden with GOLD rocks. All of a sudden I burst out laughing at the thought that I was using real gold to make the border. Remembering the Gold miners program on Tv where they would dig and dig and dig and find scrapes, and I had pounds of gold in my bucket. It was unbelievable to say the least, but I said not a word, just showed them what I wanted to do.

"What are you laughing at "? Her Mom said to me with a strange little grin on her face.

"I was remembering my Dad and his gardens all over our farm and it made me smile, that's all.

At first her mom just watched me, then slowly she and Scotia began to get it, then we were all three putting the gold around as a border. Standing back I thought we had done a great job and my smile was infectious. all could think was if I had a camera, because no one would ever believe what I had done. "Here we are" I said, a gold flower garden, not one person had a clue what that gold was worth in my time...

I really saw no flowers but I saw things that I knew were wild, because they had little wild looking blooms on them, and I dug them up and put them in their new home, probably worth six million dollars in my world. Finally as if the words were drawn from her, Scotia said the words I needed to hear, "Oh my Glenda this is beautiful,"Satisfied I had put the gold where it would stay because no one knew what it was I smiled.

"Ok girls go clean up and let's cook dinner. As we were washing I was thinking what the other members of this family would think about my rocks. I decided to wash them tomorrow. That would make them all go crazy.

Back in Scotia's room which was my room also I asked her what her mother thought. She looked at me like she didn't understand, so I said, ``Did she really like it?" All I saw was a smile, then she said "yes but she has never seen something like this before. So I had made them happy, and all I really wanted was to belong to this family until the time came and i as sent back home. All my fears had finally disappeared as I joined this strange lifestyle and felt everyday like I really belonged here with them.

I felt it and I was sort of happy and soI smiled.

CHAPTER 21

Supper was becoming a new adventure every day. Tonight I could smell something different. The smell from her kitchen was like a Turkey was cooking.

In my room I was folding the few pieces of clothes I had here and when I finished I picked them up to lay on the table and this smell was so different from laundry in my day..I had become used to washing the clothes in the stream with some bad smelling stuff her Mom put in the barrel when she washed.

I would watch them and then I would wonder how we also drank this water. I would not mention it because they had no idea what I was talking about most of the time anyway.

The man who thought he was my Grandfather was sitting on the porch as I walked up to the house. The smile was bright and he was always cherry so I said "what is that delicious smell coming from the kitchen?"

"I think it smells like the bear we put in the smoke building last season. I wondered how it could smell so good and bear meat, so I asked "What is the spice I smell from her pots"? He just looked and it was then I realised he had no idea what spice meant. So I changed the subject quickly.

Sitting down beside his old rickety chair, I stared out over this land.and I was still lonely for home but I mostly worried about Elaine. What might she be going through with my absence?

He cleared his throat, "you look worried Glenna. Again he said my name wrong. Oh well I thought to myself, who cares and most importantly it didn't make a difference. There were nights when I laid in the bed I shared with Scotia and I wondered if I would get back to my time. But it seemed to make no difference, so I tried to not think about it at all.

"I was only thinking about those gold rocks we brought back from the stream with us today. I haven't had time to even tell the others about the Diamonds I found.

He looked like I was speaking Chinese. So I changed my words to let him understand. "We also found some beautiful glass stones today," he kept staring out towards the land we were living on. I cleared my throat and he looked my way.

"Somedays I feel like I'm dancing to a tuneless song, because no one here believes me but I promise my story is accurate. He spit the tobacco juice out in the yard and came back to my side and sat down, "I believe you," he said.

I looked into his eyes and asked "how can you understand anything at all about me?" I appeared one day, you just took me in. all of you believed I was Scotia, but now everyone knows I'm not and still they make me feel like this is my home. I looked out over the land and before I knew it I said "no one would believe me if you only knew the whole story. That I'm afraid would land me out in the yard. And out of this family who took me in. I almost saw tears in his eyes. Then he said, "I know that something is not right with you. I almost think your story is true. It is very hard to hear the story and there you were. Like you appeared from nowhere. I could see he knew something, but what could it be? I moved closer to him and reached out for his gnarled old hand.

He let me take it. And I felt him squeeze my fingers. As I watched him he closed his eyes and then he began speaking.

The day you arrived here I felt something was wrong. Even though you looked like Scotia I and said you were her I knew something was different. Do you remember when I came into your room the first night?" "Yes I do, I felt that you knew I was not Scotia, and when you took my hand I felt electricity flow through our hands. I also saw it on your face. But you said nothing. So I was afraid to say anything.

He took my fingers in his. His eyes were closed. At first he said nothing but I saw the movement in his eyeballs and it moved fast to the right then to the left.

"I really do not know how to explain it but I knew then you were not like us. And my head told me to make sure you felt loved and soon our Scotia would be home with us again. I knew you had the answer but you were afraid to explain your appearance here and the way you look like our Scotia, and now we have you both, and never want to lose either one of you."He looked at me with true love in his eyes for me, and he also knew I was not from his time, but he had no way to explain it to himself let alone asking me questions. So he let my hand fall and he stared out in the vast hillside as I got up and went inside.

It was so comforting to know I was not alone here, and that he knew I was not who they thought I was.

And he never asks me questions. In the beginning when I tried to tell or explain things from my time they just did not get it so I never bring it up any more, and each person here has questions I'm so sure. But they accept me for who I am and for who I tell myself I am. What a happy feeling.

I went into the good smelling dinner that I knew was ready. It now felt like a surprise to sit down and see what it was that they made for their dinner each night. Although I sometimes did not know what she was frying, after a few questions I stopped asking and just tried it. It was 50-50 sometimes I Ate it and others I just pushed it around on my plate. And since there were mutts in the house all I had to do was act like I was loving it and carefully drop it on the floor.

After our meal we all helped clean up then we went outside to the porch area and sat around talking. I didn't talk much because I needed to listen.to learn as much as I could. As the stars came out I looked up and could not imagine how I ended up here. Going back to the Grandfather Clock in my mind I spent many an hour cussing the fact that I was looking for this and to be living the consequences of my dream was so hard to believe.

I said "I Am very tired" and looking at Scotia I could tell she was fine. So I stood up and said my good nights and went into our room.

In my sleep I heard Scotia climb in my bed. But my body was worn out and I slept on all through the night.

CHAPTER 22

W aking up to the smell of breakfast I wondered if I was the last one to wake up today. Jumping up putting on yesterday's clothes I emerged into the room and the first thing I said was "man I could eat a bear". Everyone was staring and I backed it up with a loud laugh and said "what are you cooking that woke me up smelling so good?" I saw everyone relax so I knew I had pulled off another one.

As we helped clean up the kitchen, I was amazed at the hard work just in washing dishes, we had to haul it from their well. It seems that the young people did all that bringing in the buckets for Scotia's mother. and I had not even asked about a bath for myself because so far I had not seen a single person in this house take a bath. After breakfast, Scotia and I went out back of the house and brought in several buckets for cooking and cleaning. We both were excited to go back to the little creek where I found all the gold and to the other water hole with the diamonds in it.I think it's important that I proved the diamonds were Diamonds to myself when I took big heavy rocks and tried to break them or scratch them up. So I had a healthy thing to think about now and the truth of the matter is whether I ever go home again or not,I did find these beautiful stones and they make me happy even though I don't know what the future holds. I do pray every night to return to my sister and to wake up in London to my time, and regardless of what happens this has been a thing I have lived through and I am positive that I am happy as I could be every day now. I am waiting to return but as I have no idea what happened or where I really was I also don't know when I will or if I will ever return home again.

So, the excitement of going to the stream with Scotia again made my day happy. Alone in my bed I thought about the gold and Diamonds, day and night,and it would send my brain spinning in all directions. But I always had a smile on my face,

No matter what delusion I might be suffering, the fantasy went on...

After we helped her mom clean up off we went. running out the door, her Mom said "hey girls where are you going so fast, I wanted you to bring me a bucket of cherries from the trees in the back so I can make a treat for tonight," I was looking at her face and I could tell that she had accepted me as another daughter and was still trying to make me feel the love they shared in this family, as my daily love too. Instinctively I went and gave her a hug.

I was smiling when I ran out the door with Scotia.

"Can we take a bigger bucket with us today? I thought it would be really interesting if we could bring more home to show your mother."

"of course," she said we could but then I thought about how heavy those rocks of gold were going to be and then I said "we can only bring back what we can carry easily" I saw her smile and we each carried our own bucket. I was sure our day was going to be fun. So off we went together to get Gold...or Rocks

As the days went by I became content with my life. But I never did stop thinking about how I was going to get back to the Grandfather Clock and home.

One afternoon we were carrying water to the home for Scotias, Mom when I saw a ship out in the bay area. Of course these people did not know what a Bay was, so I pointed out to show Scotia the inbound ship. She immediately began to twist her fingers. I noticed her fear was real. "Scotia, why are you afraid, because I can see it in your eyes"

"That looks like a Pirate ship, but I knew she did not know about Pirates so I took her hand and we walked closer to see whatever we could. At first I heard men, very loud men..then they spotted us. Before we could run very far they were upon us. I felt like it was a repeat of what had happened to me before. "Run to get your Mom Scotia and I will hide behind this huge jutting rock," We had ducked behind it when we first saw them coming ashore. As Scotia raced to her home she kept looking back and finally she was out of range and could not see the ship or me anymore. Out of breath she was screaming out "help us"when her father saw her running he went to see what was wrong. Out of breath she tried to explain that a ship had pulled up and that it looked like the pirate ship they found Glenda on.

Changing course the two of them ran to the house screaming "help hurry up"and the rest of the family came out. Seeing the looks on Scotia's face and her Grandfathers they went back in and got a few weapons and took off running.

She was gone, the nasty dirty pirates had gotten to Glenda before she could do anything. They tied her up and picked her up running to the ship as fast as they could. The ship was already moving out to sea when she finally pulled the smelly dirty rag they had used to capture her off her face.

They had thrown her below deck, and the motion of the ship told her that she was again lost in time. Her mind was so full of pain and loss already, but now here she was, with only her thoughts, in another time for her to accept where she might end up this time.

It felt like days had gone by. The food that was thrown down in this dark area below the deck was not good. But some days they would throw bananas down to her. She was passing the time away on the fourth day when she looked down at her dirty clothes, and then it dawned on her that as she was running she had put some of the small gold rocks in her pocket.. Feeling her pocket brought a smile to her face, and after these lost days and all the family she had lost again she was very depressed and lonely. Her heart was in pain this time, she felt like she could not go through another day all alone again, with no idea where she might end up, or even would she be able to stay alive, through all that fate could bestow on her.

CHAPTER 23

As evening fell, Glenda had already known that the dirty, nasty, murdering men on top deck were drinking alltheir alcohol getting deliriously drunk,and as time went by, all of them were growing silent, shefelt, and hoped.

So with only time on her side,she started marking the time to think if there might be the possibility of escaping the ship. All she had to do waslay low and watch the routine on the ship, day by day. And with the thought and prayers that she would endure, she laid low and tried to make plans, for the day she could escape this terrible mess she was in..

After several nights hiding below deck, It was almost like they had forgotten her. As she grew hungrier, each night, when the drunks stopped making noise, believing they were asleep, she wouldsneak up to where the food had been and scratch a bite of this or that, and stuffed some old dried out bread in her shirt pocket, so she didn't starve.

Most days were the same,then they would get close to another Island and she could hear the excitement on top of the ship, the loud boisterous voices as they got close. The next day and night she heard them making plans. She was listening and she was so amazed that they were speaking a sort of English that she could almost understand at times.

Late on the third night,she was searching through the other parts of the ship. She decided it was so big down there even in the dark that even if they heard her she could hide easily enough.

Through the long days, whenever she had time, which would be whenever she heard loud talking, she would know it was probably safe to search for food, and again when she knew they were drinking, she had also searched everywhere that she could, looking for food scraps, something, anything. Sometimes she went two or three days with nothing, but the pirates always had whiskey and water.

She wondered where they got the water they drank on the ship many times, then she decided to spy on them until she figured it out.

So early one evening she felt the ship stop, and she guessed by looking at the sun, it was maybe three o'clock. After a while she heard them get off the boat. Wondering how close they were to the land, and after checking out who was left on the ship,she sneaked up to try to see what was going on. The pirates were swimming into the beach with old brown dirty looking buckets. All of a sudden she knew they were looking for water, and they did know where the water was. Smiling to herself she took the time to look quickly for any kind of food. The only thing she found was dirty bread. But she was hungry, and she ate it as fast as she could.

And then on one particular evening after they had sort of docked this nasty piece of a ship, she decided to wait in the back until she heard no more voices. Finding a tight place to hide in she moved a big barrel and behind it she was shocked, because there was the Suit Of Armor....

Her thoughts were going crazy. What would Elaine say if I ever found her again and told her I had found the exact Armor she had explained to the smallest detail. Even a red sash bordered the arms on both sides. They were not in good condition but only the God I know, who was watching me had put me here to find it. But now, I had lost my dear sister, and I had no idea where in the world I was. When I would think that sentence I would go back to my kid years and remember saying where in the world was it? About no particular thing, but the saying made me smile anyway.

There were times like that that kept me sane. And I don't know how I knew it but I never thought I would never go back home, or even find Elaine. I just knew it through all these horrible days and nights, with almost no food or food that was already rotten, I persevered.

I scooted on my behind over to the corner where the Armor stood like a lost soldier. And when I got close enough to touch it, I thought about it long and hard, remembering the Grandfather Clock thatI had taken refuge in once a long time ago.

My brain was taking its time helping me find the right words that I could not say but I did, thinking in my mind.

How could it happen that first I had found the Grandfather Clock and then now Elaine's Armor.? Impossible was what it was, and I took the lead and scooted closer to the Huge Tall Suit Of Armor standing strong and bright in this dark corner in the boat with murderers again.

All at once I felt lost, like I had never felt before even going through all the things that I had been through. Placing both my arms around my body I began to shake, and tears came hard and fast.

Wrapping both arms around my shaking body I felt the gold rocks in one of my pockets, then when I reached in I pulled out two small rocks, about the size of a nickel. Scooting into the corner by the Armor I began to think about what else might be in one of my other holes I had purposefully stitched into my skirt.

Searching all over my body, I finally felt it cold in my pocket. Oh no, I thought it felt like the diamonds I had put in my pockets the last day we were at the waterfall. My heart started to beat so fast and my smile was proof that I had also carried a few diamonds along with the gold nuggets in my hand made pockets.

Thinking back to the time when I picked them up at the creek and put them in my pockets I had been so happy, and had no idea I would be kidnapped again, and since I didn't have but two shirts and one skirt I almost wore it every day, and on wash day I wore the pants that had belonged to a man at one time, I was sure of it.

I was in a strange mood, although the gold and diamonds made me smile when I reflected back to those happy days with Scotia, but I was lost again, and I had to not go there again. So I put on my happy face scooted over to the Suit Of Armor and touched the metal arms, then the face plate.

Thinking about Elaine's face if she could see this, was what kept me going. Her dream buy was sitting beside me. Or her dream purchase was actually standing beside me. It brought me to tears. My fears were that I would actually never get home again, and who would believe me, if I did? I was wondering if a Gene had appeared for me. Would I ask to go home, or I would ask for a polaroid camera with film!

But for tonight she was going to find something that would have to be her pencil because she wanted to try to draw the Suit Of Armor, and keep the picture if possible to give to Elaine one day.

CHAPTER 24

At this moment, I was afraid of the future again. Thinking about the actuality of being locked in the Grandfather clock, and the long days of uncertainty, then taken and captured, but so far no pain had been inflicted on her, and then escaping to find Scotia, and now I'm back on a pirate ship and captured again, it was too much to believe. Even though I was standing there with my hand on the Armor it was still like a dream. All I could think was "please I need to wake up"!

This was not possible, but here I am, my brain was on overload! After what I had been through, to even imagine it was happening again was too hard to believe, so I thought it was time to make myself calm down, take in everything I could see and hear and smell, and put together a plan of action.

So I crawled over to the closest, and darkest corner and wedged myself right beside the Armor. I was hungry and afraid of where I might end up in the morning. Oh, I was so hungry, and I was missing Scotia so much. I never expected any of this to happen to me, and I never let the thought of Elaine out of my thoughts. Where she was. And Oh God I hope nothing like this would happen to her. My brain said your sister is fine but she is waiting for some kind of a clue to help her find you.

That's how I made myself function in and through all of these positions I kept finding myself in. but I never let her sweet face get out of my mind. And I always told myself each and every day that we would find each other soon. It worked for a time.

One night I found some black coal that I was sure the pirates used to make notes or travel distances because, beside it was some old dirty rubery type of material, but not cloth at all, and I took the coal and made a mark to see if I could leave a message to my sister. Surprisingly enough it worked. It eased my mind to think that maybe someday Elaine would see this and smile.

I wrote to Elaine that I was safe and I had found her Armor. So I put it in the Armor, which was safe enough since not one time had any of those men ever been down under the ship where I was yet. So someday if we might find this Suit Of Armor that my note would be in there. when she found it. Of course these were thoughts and no reality was in the note.

But never did I think I would have been found by more pirates. After my time with Scotia I could not be that unlucky.

Even the thought right now, while I'm hiding under this dark damp tarp I found, that I would not find my way back home never entered my mind. I was absolutely certain I'd get there but only time and luck would get me there. This was something I really had to believe. I keep telling myself that everything will be fine. The whole process takes time, and from where I was sitting time was all I had.

I knew that as dark fell these men would all be very drunk and falling all over the ship, that would be my time for making a plan to get away.

Hiding down in the dark, the noises from up on the top of the ship were claiming down a lot. The voices were slurring with every word and I could hear a person just drop as they hit the deck, and passed out as I hid. My new plan was to see if I could rid the ship of some of these drunken pirates. But I had to save the Armor when I left. So that in itself was impossible.

I had to make a plan. The only thing I could think of was to kill all the pirates. But then I have not ever been the person to do such a thing. So I knew I needed a new plan. Whatever was going on I had no idea how to kill about 8 big mean grizzly dirty and drunk men.

But then I figured it out when I saw the dark black cloth laying behind the Armor. I reached back and got it, and with it my plan began to form, and it was the perfect way to hide in plain sight tonight.

I ripped three long strings and used them as the way to tie myself up, making me invisible to anyone up there who was still even a little bit sober. My heart kept telling me I was safe because the closer I got to the top of the steps, I saw no one,and there was not one man standing..Moving around silently I saw most of the eight men were asleep in a group size area. Carefully, walking and crawling around in the dark I stumbled over a bottle I found that got in my way and I grabbed it as quickly as I could, making not one sound. Moving to where I hoped I might be able to see the writing on the bottle was hard but then all of a sudden the moon came out and I saw a skull and crossbones. And a rodent. I had poison.

So in order to keep alive I knew I had to use this to survive. Moving around I found a small metal cup thinking about it, I said a big Prayer. Then I poured the poison in the cup and grabbed a broken bottle of rum and poured what was in the bottom into my cup. I started thinking about the cup as a perfect way to take care of all these horrible nasty men on here.

With that thought I decided to crawl into the corner and take a nap. Poison! It came to me all of a sudden, that I had to do my work now in the dark of night, and started making my plan.

Tonight when they were all drunk and falling asleep, I would sneak up on the top deck and do what I had to do. Thinking no more at all of actually killing these men I went about my job, knowing it was one way to get free somehow, and it never entered my mind again that I was going to murder them all.

There were rats everywhere in the night hours. I had seen them and even though they never came near a living breathing person, I had seen them, and the holes they crawled out of when they thought everyone was asleep. If rats think!

I had to be quiet, but I just wanted to laugh. This was a situation I had never thought would happen, even in a dumb dream. And I still hoped this was all a dream all except the Gold and Diamonds.

So I laid in waiting under the heavy black tarp or maybe an oil cloth,that was in a dark corner out of the way, but I could see everything that was happening even in the dark. I was getting very excited, and even knowing it might get me killed if I wasn't careful, still made me hate and want to pay them back, but now that I had a plan I would follow through even if it meant I had to kill all these nasty drunk men while they slept, And I yes I could do it.

The first thing I did when they quieted down and I heard nothing, in about half an hour, was to creep closer to get a good view, and make my plan. My head was spinning in different ways now, but I felt good about the plan and waited for dark.

It took about three hours of hiding until no one else was standing up or around and then I Could see all of them were sleeping, and snoring, and falling, wherever they happened to be standing in their drunken state, as the alcohol took over their brains.

I needed a weapon. The first thing I did was look for a knife. I kept asking myself will this work? Will I be able to kill people? And my mind said yes I had no other choice. But I had the drink and I was going to pour it in every bottle that was left with liquid in it.

One of the men was lying on his face, two other men were hanging over a barrel that had been leaning against the side of the ship.

While I was looking through these men I saw another brown bag with a skull and crossbones on the side. Picking it up felt like powder..It was more Rat poison I guessed.

I felt light headed and knew I could kill them with the knife, but the rat poison was something I could use and hide while they drank the wine and then died. But then I almost fainted from these feelings of killing the men, and realising I did not know how to sail this ship all my hopes went in the bottom of the barrel.

Oh my God I was not sure if I could kill the men or not. But what other way would I be able to get off this ship? I did not know one thing about this ship or how to sail it.

So I had another idea. I would pour the rat poison in the wine vat, and they would drink it and die that way. But again it would be me killing them. And it was certainly my only choice at the moment. But I could watch the way the ship turned or how they stopped it and have a few ideas. Still I was planning to kill ten men.

Finally I went back to the bottom and curled up next to the armor. I had a new plan. That night I decided to wait it out.

Tonight I hoped there might be another way to get free. I was worried.

So tonight I scurried back up when it was always quiet. With the spoon I had found I had my plan made. Time would tell me when to do it.

That night it was the perfect time. They were all very drunk and I sneaked up on the deck with the medicine I had made and crawled from one man to another and a spoonful went in every single mouth.

Never making a sound at all. My only hope was they would not die but be horribly sick.

This morning I still heard nothing. But I went up to check it out. To my shocked surprise I didn't find but one man and it was a young boy trying to steer the boat.

And then I walked to him, and talked with him, because I saw none of those drunk men anywhere and he looked a little lost..I asked the young boy "where are the men who were sailing this ship just yesterday?"

He told me they had all died and he threw their bodies overboard and now he was the only one left and he was only trying o get the boat to a dock. But he said, "nothing that looked like land anywhere was in sight yet."

She saw the frightened look on the boys face and asked him his name, he said my name is Al, they talked then one afternoon one day later as they had tried to sail the ship, and not knowing where to go, they saw a ship was coming up to the side of our ship and then in the bottom of this odd ship I heard screaming and the boat was lurching, and I ran back down in the far corner by the armor. I motioned for him to come too. I climbed in as fast as I could and hid. For hours there was screaming and I heard gunshots, and then something bumped the boat and shook me so hard that I tried to climb out of the metal suit. All at once the boat tipped over and the armor fell to the side with me in it. I stayed quiet and didn't move a muscle. Time went by and there was not a sound up over my head. I stayed still and after a long time I heard the feet running all over the ship, and then coming down to the underside where I was. Quietly I laid still, the men were obviously searching for something because the time they were searching went by slowly, and then after what felt like hours, they left. Quiet was a hard thing to get used to, after the screaming and shots and tramping all over my head. Still I stayed where I was. As the night started to fall and the darkness fell into the bottom of the boat and there was not a sound anywhere. So I carefully crawled out of the Armor and tiptoed up to see if anyone was there. It was so quiet and hearing no feet or seeing anyone made me feel safe and I tiptoed around, still alerted by any simple sound. Knowing that every minute counted I rushed faster. There was not one person on the boat. Only me.

I was not afraid, but now my heart was beating so fast and so hard, because even though I knew I did not know how to steer a boat, or guide it, or whatever needed to be done, I knew it was me against whatever would come my way.

But knowing I could not do it alone, was hard to accept, as the fear had built up in me, but as I got close to realising it, I also felt my brain get strong and as the minutes went by, I knew I could do this, and I had to do it.

So I walked to the right side, on the top of the boat and sat down leaning my head against the rough boards.

Maybe ten minutes went by, in the twilight and erie calm seas, and still no one was there.

Just as I was falling asleep I thought I heard a voice calling out so I kept quiet, not moving a muscle.

Then I heard it again. I straightened up, peeking up. I saw a very young boy, guessing maybe twenty years old, how old for sure I didn't know. He had blood all over his face. And he was crying silently to himself. Still I waited. Then after about thirty minutes he went silent and the crying stopped. He called out to anyone if they heard him to please come help him. I could tell he was not sure if anyone was there. I knew he needed help, and needed me but I was still afraid that he might be one of the Pirates that didn't die, and I waited maybe five minutes looking everywhere to see if anyone was there to help him, and when no one came to help him, I saw him fall over a big wooden platform of some kind. He was crying very hard but not loud at all. His eyes were searching for help. She could tell that.

After a few more minutes he was silent. At first she thought he might have died. And dread filled her brain.

And that scared her very much, but then she heard him again. So then she thought that he probably needed her, and might have seen her and was waiting for her to show herself.

The crying went on and on. And the sobbing broke her heart. She kept thinking "but what can I do?

So she stood up and inched quietly toward where she had seen him at first, before he fell when he was standing. He was lying on the dirty floor boards, and as she got closer to the sobbing. It took all her calm and she began to see his body laying almost at her feet now. He looked up and seemed to be trying to turn and run, when he said please don't leave me all alone here.

I turned back around and I saw a young man there. Maybe barely fourteen or fifteen years old I was guessing.

CHAPTER 25

So now that I knew or felt sure that I was probably alone on the ship, I pushed through the debris and went over to him, and not wanting to frighten him I quietly said, ``What has happened here to you?" Then she walked over closer to him.

He looked up at me and I saw a piece of dirty, bloody jagged wood about eight inches long from the entry point and out to the top, deeply embedded in his arm real close to his shoulder bone, I knew I could help him but with these dirty floors and that piece of wood probably covered with germs, and maybe already putting poison into his body, it took my breath away for a few seconds and then my brain took over.

I smiled and he said "It hurts" and I felt that he was a good boy, maybe trapped here, as I was.

After I had already singlehanded poisoned all those men, I realised at that moment that I was a much stronger person, so I stopped down near his face. Calmly I said "if you will let me I can help you". He closed his eyes and shook his head yes that I could help him. Then I heard him say "Please, I am not one of those bad men, I am swearing it to you."

First I had to think about how I could help him. So I began to speak very slowly and kept my voice calm and quiet. "I'm not a Doctor but I do know I need to get that bit of wood out of your arm" waiting to see how he would interpret what I had said, I brushed his long brown hair out of the way so I could see if this was something I could do or not. "Let me go find some water and I'll wash this off and when we can see how far it is in your arm, then I will know what to do for you" she saw him smile a tiny smile, then he closed his eyes, from fear or pain she was not too sure.

At first I thought what if he had died, then I thought I had better hurry up and get busy trying to find some cloth of some kind and string and maybe a bottle of whisky which I knew there were many bottles on this ship, but probably empty, so I searched. Actually I had seen a big wooden crate with clear liquid in it and It looked like some kind of alcohol, just the night before,because I had almost tripped over it.

It didn't take me long to find some cloth and a big knife to cut it with, I hurried back to his side. He was now unconscious. I thought this definitely would be better for both of us.

Running back to the boy, first I cut the shirt off with the ragged knife I found,then I poured some of the whiskey on his cut. His body clenched and he jerked.

As the liquor wet the shirt, and he did not wake up, I touched the piece of wood and itfelt like it was not in his flesh, so after I got it wet enough it almost fell out and I did not have to hurt him. I tried to clean the wound the best I could, but because I was afraid he would wake up and scream or cry, I was not sure if I got it clean enough. The blood was flowing, and then as I poured more alcohol on it, it did slow down. The boy was still out and that was good.

I ran all around looking for a piece of cloth to wrap around it. Finally I saw some material laying on a little bunk like bed.and grabbed it and ran back to bind the cut and try to stop the bleeding.I dipped it in the water over the side of the boat many times, I knew it was still dirty but it was all I had, and time was flying by, and I Didn't want him to wake up til I had it bandaged.

CHAPTER 26

About an hour had gone by and he opened his eyes. He immediately looked at his arm. Seeing the bandage and the piece of wood gone he looked up at me and smiled, "how did you do that" then I told him the wood got wet and just fell out, and it was not a deep cut at all, and not to worry. I made him comfortable and then I asked him if he knew how to sail the boat? At first he said he thought he could because he was put on the other ship to learn the ways of the Pirates.

But he did not want to be there, they had made him, and he had seen the many bad things they did, and then they treated him so terribly, and all he really wanted was to go home to his mother. Soon he fell asleep.

She went looking for some water. Cool clean water Since it was their only source for drinking, she knew there would be some somewhere, and they would be ok. There was all kinds of homemade alcohol, but not water, and they had been so drunk some nights as she hid in the deepest darkest part of the ship for hours, or until they became quiet.

Soon she found water. Searching through all these things she finally found water and a wooden cup which she filled with water, and heading back to the boy she even took a sip for herself. When she got to him he was looking for her.

"Here you go let me try to help you get a big drink" he tried to sit up and then he told her the pain was gone and he wanted to thank her.

She smiled and went to a more important question.

A question that would take a lot off her mind and help them get the heck out of there.

"Ok, Are you ready to repay me for my surgical experience? all the while watching his eyes.

"So how do we steer this boat?" Watching his eyes, she saw him give a tiny smile, I'm sure you can see I'm not the Captain. She was smiling.

And she could tell that he thought he knew how to help her get them out of this Innlet. They were parked in the funny word Innlet!

He said he knew how, because he had always been on the boats with his father since he was 3 years old. The smile on his face made her smile back. So now, with the right coxing, maybe she could get him to steer it away from this cove and find a place where they could wait to be rescued,or maybe into a dock where they could escape. She couldn't help thinking about her loneliness and how many days and tests she'd been forced to go through so far.

From that day so long ago, now in her mind, with Elaine in the antique shop, now feeling like it was so long ago. To this barbaric ship with murderers and being lost again. Just last night she had dreamed she was back with Scotia and her family, only to wake up on this horrible Pirate ship. Pirate Ship was all she could think of to call it. Because in her young years she had nothing to compare it to.

As the days went by with her companion, and new friend, they together learned how to move the ship and move it fast. The wind pushed them out into the sea, and at first she was afraid that he might get them lost and end up back in trouble. She did not want another chance to be captured again.

Within two days her new friend was moving about as if he was never hurt at all. She was very proud of her nursing skills, and the boy's fast recovery. But most of all how she takes care of things that she never knew about before. Not even the fact that his wound was not getting infected was a miracle in itself.

At one point as she was sitting beside him as he steered their ship away, they talked about her escape from the other Pirates many months ago. He was very interested and she felt so proud of herself for being so clever and surviving all these terrible things that had happened to her.

So she told him about the Gold, and Diamonds.

Together one evening as they made a plan for the day to come, she asked him if he wanted to see her treasures of gold and Diamonds. He actually had no idea what she was talking about, and she knew it, so she decided it would be a great subject for one evening as they ate the few fish they had been able to catch off the side of the boat.

"I want to show you my things I brought with me when I had to leave Scotia and her family.

Immediatley he looked shocked and asked her "why did you have to leave your home?"

I was trying to think how to explain this to him. But no words came that would make sense at all.

"I will try to explain it to you later, but not now.I want to show you something else, I think you will love to see my rocks."

Using the word rocks was a way I could show him first, and then see what he had to say and what he thought about the so-called rocks. I was not sure if I should ask him how he ended up on the ship from the beginning or leave it alone, so for now I didn't ask.

Then I said, "one day Scotia and I were washing some clothes for her mother and I put my feet in the water."

Trying to cool off in the water, and there were hard rocky feeling things hurting my feet, so I reached down and picked them up and that's when I saw the shiny gold rocks.

And then the next week Scotia told me she knew a different part of the stream where there were even prettier rocks, and when she said they were sort of clear I asked her to take me there and we gathered some of up and took them to her home with us, I know what they are but, here she stopped talking so not to make her look stupid.

His eyes were shining with curiosity but he didn't say anything. "Well, do you want me to go get them?"

His face took on a happy look and she could already tell he was excited to see them, so she said "hold on", and he looked at her as if she was speaking a different language. She asked him "what was that look on your face" then she laughed.

With a strange look on his face he said, "What do you mean hold on"? and the look on her face told him maybe she didn't understand him? She thought this slang was so funny. Her everyday slang threw him for a loop. Then she started to explain it

Laughing silently to herself she told him that when she said hold on a minute, she only meant that if he could wait a minute. She saw the smile on his face. Her happiness radiated from her to her new friend.

"You know some days you say the strangest things he said with his eyebrows raised, and I try to understand but you are really talking in strange ways, but then when you tell me what you meant "I do understand".

The look on his face told Glenda that he had more questions, but so far he had kept them to himself.

After rumbling around in the dark of the ship she found the dirty old sock where she had put the Gold and Diamonds. Climbing back up the rickety rough made steps with her treasure she had pasted a huge smile on her face. Pouring the treasure for him to see, and to touch gave him a happy glow about his eyes.

Holding out his hands, she saw the astonishment on his face. Almost like shock.

"I have never seen these kinds of rock before," he told her. She could see him marvel at the beauty of the Gold. rough and dirty. Then when she pulled out the Diamonds his face went ashen. "What's wrong?" she asked him.

Reaching towards his arm she touched him and she could feel him shaking. With no idea what was wrong she stepped back a few steps and waited for him to speak.

Finally he said "I used to keep lots of rocks in my room at my homestead. She could hear the loneliness in his words.

It made her shiver with concern about her own outcome here, but never did she quit working towards her home. "But since I left, I now have nowhere to go, but

I'm sure I will keep my mind clear, and at the end of this I will find a new homestead."

She saw him try to smile. It made her heart warm to know that she was there and would keep him safe and as happy as they could be together. Since now she knew they were both now lost to their own time.

The days went by slowly but they were content and every day as they watched and searched the coastline, and searched everything that went by them for signs of land that would be safe for them to land and look for people, and safety.

The morning breezes pushed them out and as the days went by they became like a brother and sister.

Glenda was still sad to have lost Scotia. Day after day the memories come and go. But on the other hand, she knew she had been so very happy with her experience. As the days went by she still missed her friendship and even the family that belonged to Scotia, that had taken her in, had also been missed.

CHAPTER 27

Today they knew they needed to find some land, because even though they had tried to find food, and they had fished a few mornings when they needed food, it was not good enough. But the fishing was not good. She had tried to find a fish hook but had no luck. Or any kind of wire. They needed something to make into the shape of a hook. She had tried to explain it to Al but he just did not get it.

So after talking about it they started to turn the ship, so the wind would blow them in the direction of the closest point of land, so that they could put the ship into and climb off.

As they got close to the land they saw people running out of the trees to see who was coming.

And they hand held dangerous items, they could hurt and kill with.

From the yelling and the faces full of hate they knew they only had a couple of minutes to turn around and get the heck out of there.

The wind was blowing southwesterly and they headed into it and the boat took off away from the dangerous men running out to try to get them and the boat.

"Al, this was a scary moment, but the wind saved us this time".

Running to the back of the boat to make sure no one was coming after them, there was no one in sight. They had escaped again.

Not far from there, they pulled their new home, the ship into a hiding place that was so green and the trees were hiding the ship enough that they felt safe to get off and hunt for a rabbit or anything they could cook and eat. "I'm a really good hunter," Al said as he saw she had a frightened look on her face. "She rubbed her stomach, then looked toward him, and saw him laughing, and then he reached down and rubbed his own stomach, "I hope so because we both need food or anything we can find to get us out to the other side where the sea has a lot of food in there for us.

Slowly, watching every angle, they entered the cove. And since it was almost dark she said "let's pull in here" pointing to a thick stand of trees and piled up brush that looked like it washed in from a terrible storm, "and lay low until after dark falls so we can smell firewood, or see if anyone is on this island, and then we can make a fire for tonight, and hunt tomorrow for food to take us on the rest of our journey."

Slowly, looking so nervous, he backed the ship into an easy spot, big enough to get out of fast if the need arrived, and also they were hidden from most eyes, by overgrown trees and brush piled up on both sides where the tide dumped everything after storms passed, then he asked her "please tell me how do we lay low"?

Shaking her head, and covering her mouth, she laughed hard but told him that was what people did when they were hiding from someone.

Seeing him repeat those words "hiding from someone" he shook his head, yes.

Promising that he was wanting to learn a lot of new phrases from her, and when they found a safe place someday soon he would be talking like her.

She saw him looking at her, and he shook his head yes, with a beautiful smile. And it was then that she first noticed what a handsome boy/man he had become in their short time alone, together. She felt like she needed to be a mother to him and she absolutely knew what it felt like to be so alone, so from now on she decided to mother him, and knew it would be good for him, because she really wanted him to feel what she had felt when Scotia's mother had mothered her, and as she needed it she also knew he needed her now too. Together they would make a good team and soon find a safe haven to begin another life.

Looking out to sea, her mind wondered how many more times was she going to be lost before she instantly returned home to real life.

As the evening cloud wore on and as the dark fell all over the island, their ship was hidden, and seeing they jutting out just enough for them to have space enough to back into it, they felt safe, then they could outrun anyone who came looking, dangerous or like a threat to them.

Through these past days, and now weeks together, they were comfortable with almost anything that could come up and everything that had come up so far.

"Iam hungry," she said loudly. And laughing Al said he had a plan that would feed them. Talking steadily he told her he had hidden a few weapons after he threw the dead bodies overboard, for safety, and protection. He mentioned that he did not know she was there yet, so he had put it in the back of his mind for another time.

"We should go hunting for our food while we have the chance" She was listening.

"I'm ready, and I think I saw some rabbits playing right over there a while ago" Pointing towards a group of trees. Running back behind her to a big pile of what looked like trash to her, she heard him rummaging in something. Turning all the way around she heard him but again did not see him. Walking towards the noise he jumped out from under a pile of trash, and scared her pointlessly.

In his hand he had a weapon. Seeing her expression he commented that when she first found him that day, he had hidden a long sword and gun from her for his protection. After he realised she was his friend, he forgot about them, because so far they had not needed any weapons to keep them safe.

To her surprise, there he stood, and he had two big long nosed pistols in his hands and a sword hanging on his roped belt. And some kind of a needle nosed looking thing hanging on his other side.

At first she was just speechless. She just stood there staring. Then came the amusement and the laughter came bubbling out of her mouth.

"Where on earth did you get those Al?" looking shocked, and still smiling she said I can't believe it. When he told her, she smiled thinking he was smarter than she imagined. He had dug them up from down under the boat, when one afternoon he had wandered down there hoping he might find another shirt, when he saw it in a barrel he examined it deeply and found weapons that put a huge smile on his cheerful face. Thinking they might need them in the next part of their travels he decided to wear them and surprise her. That morning the boy had a new look on his face of satisfaction, he certainly had surprised her.

She felt a chilling feeling that he had known this but didn't tell her, and what else did he know, was he afraid of her from the first? And even though they both sat down and began to examine the precious find, first picking up one then another, realising she had no idea how any of these work, and of course there were no bullets here in this time frame, "when did you think to look for these guns, and how long have you known these were here Al?"

He smiled and said he took them from the dead mens bodys, before he threw the bodies overboard.

He had thought about it for a long time, and then he had hidden them in case he needed protection on his travels, knowing that being alone on the ship was dangerous and he was so glad he had watched how the now dead pirates, handled the ship pulling in and out of places as they pulled into to find food and fresh water, and now he was so glad he been watching the men because he had been in the bottom of the ship most days, so he knew nothing about how to steer the ship that first morning. But he had been watching them for a long time and had a good feeling about what he was doing.

And in his mind, so since he was the man here he had to keep her safe.

Together they practiced with the guns and learned how to load and unload and then the afternoon was over and they both were hungry.

"What can we eat Al?" His smile lit up his face, and he rubbed his stomach and took her by the hand over to the corner of the boat, where he had a dirty old bucket sitting there with a piece of a dirty brown cloth over it. She looked at him and then he removed the cloth showing her a big fish with his head cut off. She smiled at AL and could not believe what she saw. "When did you get this Al?" Her expression of disbelief was amazing. He said "I got up early this morning and I saw you sound asleep, so I took the hook I found stuck in the boards where I was laying a few days ago. And I was so hungry all I wanted was food, and after scurrying around I found a string that was stuck on the floor and I made myself a fishing line. When this big fish started to nibble on my line I knew we would have breakfast today!" her smile made it all worth well for him.

They decided to clean it and cook it, but she thought, if we only had a refrigerator we could save the rest for tomorrow. But by now it was evident this time she might be stuck here for who knows how long?

As the sun started to fade into evening, and the sun dipped lower as evening, they were both content with their meal and now they put a blanket in the corner of the ship and both sat down to enjoy the gentle movement of the ocean and the feeling of fullness and contentment for now.

They both felt a contentment that was rather new to them both, they had survived so many trials, so far and Al had no idea how many times Glenda's world had changed and thrown her into new frightening times and places, and but they spent time talking and discussing their next move and where they might end up as they neither one had any idea how to read the compass, and charts that were left by the front end. "I remember reading somewhere that people can use the stars to guide them, but as for today and the two of us we do not know a thing about the stars. As each evening ended, and after they had some sort of food, maybe fruit they both gathered when they docked at an known shore that looked safe and there was no sign of any people they would enjoy there spoils for the day, and they both would crawl down under the worn and dirty old piece of fabric which they had torn into two pieces a long time ago, and their sleep was always quick and ended too soon.

CHAPTER 28

The days went slowly by as they planned their next Adventure. Hoping to find another place to dock so they could hunt for food, both of them were eager to get on land again..And one morning Al asked her "how long do you think we have been out here"?

It was times like these when she remember the comforts of her own home, and mourn their loss.

Her days were passing by with their own little bits of pleasure, like the fruit they would gather together when they came into sight of land where no one seemed to be living. It made their days happy as they could be, and they would gather whatever was on the branches or the hard old ground. It brought them a peaceful relationship, and they kept each other content while on this weird journey. There were times she wanted to try to explain things to him but it felt like he was not ready to hear it or talk about things unknown to him.

And so the days went by. Always fishing, or gathering fruit if it came into sight, and passing the long summer days sometimes were a blessing. They were safe

Sitting on a huge old branch.waiting for Al to come back with something for them to eat, she was thinking about the pain she had been through since the beginning of this nightmare. Looking around the area that AL had chosen to steer the boat into, she could tell he had them hidden from all possibilities of eyes, possibly seeing their boat and attacking them.

She heard an explosion off to her left, and kept her eyes riveted in that area, when she saw All coming toward the boat she wanted to be able to help him if he had had any luck finding them food. Thinking about being adrift in time was not something anyone would ever think of, let alone to be there, and not knowing what tomorrow might bring made her feel like her existence in general was not safe.

Dailey, she told herself she had to be dreaming, but pinching her arm time and again she realised she was there, even though she did not know where she might be, the experiences she had gone through were far from a dream. There was the part about the Gold she had found, and the murders she had committed, knowing that, made this so real and altogether unbelievable.

The evening was coming and the sunset was a perfect picture. Al had just climbed back on and so the topic was food. "What can we eat tonight Al?"

"I have a surprise for you," he replied,reaching into his deep pockets in those incredibly baggy and worn out pants that she had seen him in for the whole time they had been together, he pulled out berries, to her they looked like blackberries, but when he handed her one and she took a bite she found it was so sour that it took her breath away, however being in her mouth she changed the look on her face to a smile and actually the more she chewed the better it tasted. Realising that she was so hungry she would almost eat anything, except another nasty fish, that was why they had stopped fishing, because it had become boring.

Her smile was infectious and when he asked her why the big smile she replied "this sad dinner for us when I have gold and diamonds in my pack in the bottom of the boat." they both laughed and collapsed to the deck rolling around.

"AL in the morning I have an idea for us to check out if you don't mind," He just looked at her and his curiosity won over, with his question, "is your surprise food?" she told him she had been thinking and that tomorrow she wanted them to both get off the boat and check out the surroundings and if it was safe they needed to explore inland a bit further". His face lit up and then he asked her what and where she intended to go".

"I want to find fresh water for us first and then follow this water looking for more gold and or diamonds"!

She saw the surprised look on his face. Continuing.

"And if we decide we are safe here we could explore and maybe find some food and if we run into a home and it is deserted, who knows what we might find for ourselves. "she then saw his look and it was no secret he was not happy with her idea. Then he spoke up in the big moment she had been waiting for with his fears and explaining their danger. She showed him a smile and resaid everything that he needed to hear to get the idea also.

"We might come across a deserted house, and in it there might be a blanket, or clothes, or a pan and some dishes for us.

So, with a smile, he finally said it sounded like a good direction for them in the morning. That evening they cooked a small piece of squirrel meat they had killed a few days ago.There was nothing else for them to eat tomorrow and he knew it was time to bring in food now. His smile brightened.

Bringing their boat back in from the reef they were sitting on this day, he turned it around to find a lush green covered spot that had them out of sight they both got the boat snug into a little cove, under the cover of many twisted and gnarled vines, and greenery that almost actually hid them from sight. The feeling of safety was almost as necessary as food. So this evening they slept well with a small dinner and with thoughts of tomorrow and what they might find.

She went to the corner where they kept those nasty things she called blankets and together they folded them out and the best part of the evening arrived. The boat was hidden and they were safe enough to really sleep well. They did not have these nights often and they were both so very tired, but they hadn't thought about that previously.

Each night had brought many situations that they had grown accustomed to, so tonight as both of them shook out the dirty ragged blankets they had been using for a long time, she looked at Al and smiled as if to say tomorrow will bring us good luck.

There hadn't been many days or nights with perfect endings, to night was a perfect example to show Al

That things could change at any moment and this was one of them.they both found the perfect place to sleep tonight and soon she heard him snoring softly, which was rare.

The birds woke them up with the first light. Stretching from a good solid quiet night's rest. Both of them felt the excitement of another adventure. And feeling safe was not something they had felt in a long time.

Yawning and fluffing her hair which was so dirty she even smiled at that. He came over where she was sitting and said to her, "I'm ready, let's go."

She saw a sparkle of excitement in his demeanor today. Not something she had seen in this long friendship.

Late in the night she had thought out a simple plan and even imagined they might meet new people who might take them in and feed them, but that would be seen.

The sun was hot this morning, so she took her dirty blanket and tried to wash it a bit. Dipping it in the water over the side of the boat the water turned black. She was grossed out completely and also satisfied that even a little dunking was better than nothing.

Al saw her and came over to see what she was doing. "You are cleaning your blanket, and if it doesn't get dry today I'll let you have mine. If it gets dry in the morning you can help me clean mine. He had his hand on his hips and was smiling showing white teeth. That shocked me. The dental hygiene here did not exist. But I had never noticed his teeth before, always thinking they were rotten as most of the people I had come in contact with here had shown me, he had white teeth, and I loved it that he was happy enough to give a smile that big about our plan for today.

The day felt different somehow, I was sure it was because we had together made a plan for today last night and had something fun to do today. Indeed unless we ran into something bad our day was going to be the first perfect one so far for both of us.

As we climbed over the side making sure not to move our cleaned blankets out of the beautiful warm early sun, we headed off for today's adventure, and unless we found people and had to recoup our plans, We could have the first day of pleasure for both of us.

Walking and not talking until we found the path was clear, and after about thirty minutes I said "you know what I miss more than anything from my real life? At once I saw him frown. "Have you never wondered where I came from? Or how did I get here"?

He just looked, and with a sigh of relief he told me his thoughts, and I then knew he was a very private person, who asked no questions and waited to see what the person he was with wanted to freely tell him. And of course I had had no time to enlighten any of those people who I had been thrown in with throughout this time in my life.

To me it felt like, as the days went by and the circumstances changed I had to go with the flow. From the first days in the Antique store when I saw my Grandfather Clock, everything had been one challenge after another. Waking up inside the huge old clock to find myself a captive and then Scoticia and now Al, it was almost more than I could bear, those memories had not dimmed but there had been so many times, I did not think they would, and now here I was with Al and it was so sad that he was so young and his life was empty. I decided to question him about his life and parents as soon as we had a quiet time. Today, since I had prayed last night for the chance to find more information about him and also share what I felt like he might be able to grasp if the time was right, if not today then another time as it appeared as if I was here for good. That made me sad and the lonely feelings returned. I was almost thinking about telling him about Elaine and how this got started. But I knew he couldn't grasp the concept at all and it would all be so confusing to him, and I changed my mind.

We had walked a long time, being quiet and watching out for predators and or people who might help us.

Knowing it was not feasible and the idea was only an idea I did not bring up anything to confuse my friend. All at once Al turned around and reached for my hand and put his fingers to his mouth as if saying do not talk, and then I heard water moving at a rapid pace. He turned and said "where there's water there will be people."

He was right and I suddenly got worried about the two of us, there we were alone with only one long blade knife.

We squatted down in the trees and sat there just watching. The people we saw seemed to be a family with about five little kids.

The mother was washing and scrubbing some things on a huge rock that looked as if she had been using this same rock a long time.

We got under a huge vine and scooted up into the branches. All I could think about was spiders. But Al assured me he did not see even one. That's when I whispered and told him about my phobia over spiders. I saw his mouth twist into a smile but he kept quiet, making sure we were not overheard and keeping us safe, until he thought it ok for us to move on.

Soon the family picked up the clothes and headed back to their home I assume. It was strange, because they were carrying all the clothes in their arms. Reminding me about my laundry baskets, and wishing I could invent them for these people. When they were out of sight we moved down the steep hill trying not to get tangled up in the branches. We waited probably thirty minutes and we did not hear a sound, only water flowing down the bank from where we were hiding.

I do not know when the idea hit me, but the sound of the water lulled me into thinking we were safe so I told AL to come down stream, pointing where all those big trees were, and let's look for gold and or more diamonds.

He smiled and shook his head and told me to stay where I was while he made a search of this area to make sure we were safe to go splashing in the water. I sent him a smile and shook my head ok. The stream was really wide but not too deep all the way across to the other side. The two of us got down in different places and I had explained how I had found them before when Scotia and I were doing laundry, and another time when we just splashing around in the water and they were hurting my feet.

For a long while we saw nothing, then I picked up a sharp stick that immediately put about six or seven long splinters in my fingers. I cried out keeping as quiet as I could, and Al came running to my side, it only took a few minutes to pick them out and they were not in there bad.

It felt like we had been there for a long time, and the sun was going down so I knew we had to get back to the ship and make sure we were not seen. It seemed an easy return but what if we got lost.

I had many worries and when I mentioned them to Al he said he followed the path of the sun and he could retrace our steps easily. That made me smile.

Just as we climbed up the bank to head back to the boat I grabbed a hold of a sharp rock sticking out of the dirt and fell down toward the water. My hands slipped and I fell down into the deep, cold, water. It was only about knee deep, which was good for us,and while I was scrambling for a foot hold I felt sharp rocks under my feet. I told Al to help me pick some up, and he came right in and got big hands full of dirt to look through. We found the gold again. They were tiny but they were gold.

"So please tell me, why do you think they are so great?' again I had the feeling that gold was not so important yet, in this world, and maybe I should forget all about it.

"Well where I come from gold is a way to get money, to buy things we need to survive, in the way we have been used to."

"Ok I really am not sure what you mean but I think we need to gather a lot of them for our use as we leave this area."

Feeling better, together we both got into the water and found many pieces of gold. Looking for the diamonds like I found with Scotia, in a different little river of water was not so here. We found none and after about an hour we decided to get back to the ship, the sun was low in the sky and even though I had no idea what time it might be, I did know we needed to hurry, and we did just that.

The wild growth all around us still amazed me day after day and today was no exception.

As we walked back to the ship I thought it was maybe 6:00 because I could see the sun low in the sky. And always I had the fear someone might come upon our ship and try to steal it. And that would mean possible they would kill us, so we were so very careful, and quiet as we approached the spot we had hidden the ship in, at that moment in time I would never have been any happier, because there she sat, waiting for her time travelers to come aboard.

Maybe it was the sweltering heat, or the mile I had walked, whatever it was I was decidedly exhausted.

Being outdoors so long and walking to find the little creek had taken its toll on me. I asked Al how he felt, he turned to look at me and asked me why I asked him that? "I'm really tired," is all I said. "Why don't you take a rest for a few hours as I try to get us back on course"?

That sounded good to me and it still amazed me when he never asked any questions, or trid to get me to explain myself in any situation we had found ourselves in.'

My thoughts were, yes people can change, and I had been through so many things, and I most certainly had changed with each encounter in my time traveling. Just thinking those words made me think that someday when I got back to my time and my sister, I would write it all down, and so I needed to keep things clear in my mind, to keep my memory clear on the exact things that had happened to me.

Sleeping hard we never knew when the pirates boarded our ship, then the noise woke us up. I was under the deck, but Al happened to be on the top deck.

It must have been midnight, and we both were running to get our guns, but there were all over the ship by the time we finally heard them, and I felt the ship take a blow from something bigger than us, all I could think was oh God here we go again. And my brain said maybe this is how you get back to your time and Elaine, so be careful and do whatever they ask.

I ran towards Al who was already in chains all around his legs and arms.. Where did the chains come from I wondered?

I stood still and tried to ask them what was going on, but not one man spoke to me. They ignored me as if I was not even there. I remembered someone slammed me down in the back of the ship, and so I remained quiet trying to get my bearings, and to hear them talking, I needed to know what language they were using.

Knowing I had to get off the ship and fast, my mind went to the gold and diamonds I had hidden below. I suddenly realised it was actually close and easy to grab. So I did get it before I made any more decisions on my next dilemma. Climbing back up, all was clear, it seemed the pirates had more things to do and had forgotten about me.

I remember seeing Al motioning me back, but I had wanted to get the gold/diamonds.I don't know when that came to my mind but it did, I wanted to get my bag of gold and diamonds no matter what.

I had stumbled and crawled down to get my gold. So I stood still and looked for a place to hide. Silently I worked my way to the end of the ship and quietly I lowered myself into the water and made my way to the shore and safety, quietly with not a single splash,with a bag of gold and diamonds, all of a sudden I saw Al was not in sight any more.

My brain kept saying what are you waiting for? So I swam slowly and not making a single sound crawled out of the murky water and searching

I found the perfect hiding place, and hid in the tall dense grass until the light of the day showed me the activity on board. I kept searching for Al. but he was nowhere to be seen. And the fear they would jump in the water and come after me told me to slip as far away as I could get, as fast as I could.

I remembered the last time I saw Al and he'd motioned his head to the end of our boat and made the words "Jump quietly" then he moved his mouth to say "NOW" just remembering this was sad.

I found a mound of ground that had a small space under all the dirt and rocks, and I dug myself in tight. That is where I waited for nightfall, and then after a few hours went by all of a sudden I heard nothing. It had been loud and then it was like they were gone. I waited a few more hours silently, then as the sun started to dip into the water Icrawled out of my hiding place to crawl as close as I could I could get but when I had retraced my steps I was sickened to see the ship gone. And the pirate ship was also gone. That told me they had taken our ship and the other half of the pirates had followed them as they took our ship out into the deep water and disappeared.

I was thankful for the daylight so I crept back to where I had been hiding. It was almost impossible for me to believe this had happened to me again. I could not get my brain into mode "think" so I curled up in the brush and cried. "Why God"? "I want to go home, I need to find my sister and please tell me why this keeps happening to me. Oh God I used to think I was dreaming and I would wake up, but it didn't ever happen.

How could this happen again I wanted to know. I cried myself to sleep.

CHAPTER 29

When I woke up it was another day and I knew it was time to get moving and so I walked as close to the edge of the water that I could for hours. Never seeing anyone or another boat or even a bird in the sky. My mind kept saying how could this keep happening to me, but I could not answer.

Laying down in the sweet smelling grass I decided to get up and walked and walked. Hours went by when I found a hidden area that was covered up by the brush and I investigated. I noticed I was close to water again and I fell down in the hole and cried some more. Falling asleep fast left me no more time to think. Time after time I rolled over and just gave up.

Somewhere in my sleep I thought I heard someone calling my name. It was Elaine, she was sobbing.

I jerked upward. My surroundings were familiar and my brain said "look up you are home".

I was not in the bushes anymore, I was laying on a street up against a big wall. and The first thing I thought was, this is the best nightmare I ever had, and then, have I returned to London? Is this nightmare over? People were staring at me. I was dirty, I was starving, and I was crying.

Some policeman came over to me and asked me if I needed help.I tried to stand up, they helped me. I eagerly reached into my pockets and my bag was still there My gold and diamonds were with me. In shock this was unbelievable, as the police man or Bobby as they called them here, lifted me upward. I asked him if he could take me to our hotel. My prayers were all I had to keep me going. I told him the name and he gently put me into his car and we rushed through the early morning traffic in midtown London.

At first I was silent. Then I asked the man driving if he could tell me the date, because it felt like a year had gone by since I had disappeared, but I just knew Elaine was still there waiting for me.

We pulled up to the hotel and they helped me out of the police car and into the lobby of this fancy hotel. The looks and stares did not even phase me. So as I I waited for the policeman to get the room number, which I gave him from memory, but he asked anyway, so as if to prove I was not a nut case. I asked him to please hurry. Up the elevator we went. As we got to the door he knocked loudly. I noticed he was exchanging looks with the other policeman, but in five seconds he swung open the door and there was Elaine, she looked like she was going to faint. Grabbing me into her arms she didn't give me time to speak before she jumped me for answers

The gang at the door turned and left us alone. After a while I figured out I had been gone more than a month.

The first thing I told her was do not ever go looking for your Suit of Honor again. "I found it and I also found the Grandfather Clock. Her expression changed into delight...she said thanks to the policeman and almost closed the door on his big nose.

She said, "you have been gone for a long time, then she stopped and looked me over and took me into her arms, saying "I need to get you in the bath, and i'll order food then we will tuck you into the bed and after you rest we will talk.

"My God I had begun to think that all the policemen might be right, that you went off somewhere to get away from me. And some person had murdered you. But no matter how many times I told them what had happened they most certainly did not ever believe me."

I could tell she was in shock. I didn't talk anymore

I asked her to sit by the tub while I cleaned up and I also took my bag out of my pocket and laid it in her hands. She looked at it and asked me what it was.

"Please open it and then maybe you won't have so many questions, but you will certainly have new questions for me.

I'll watch and soak here and when you are ready I do have a tale to tell you."

She nodded her head and kept taking my hand as if to make sure this wasn't a dream.

There was a knock at the door, which was food. I almost cried when I saw the scone and jam.

I began to talk and eat and at the same time, and I kept reaching for her hands, to reassure me I was back where I belonged. She gave me pitiful looks and many smiles and a lot of questions, which she didn't give me time to answer.

After I got out of the tub and put on my soft wonderful smelling robe and gown I crawled into the bed. With her sitting there by me I began to tell her a story that no one with a brain would have been able to believe.

The first thing she did while I cramped a fresh warm scone filled with clotted cream into my mouth was to pick up the bag and shake it then she had a million questions for me. "Please Elaine, I need you to open the bag and then I will try to explain.

Her fingers were trying hard but I had tied it twenty times trying to keep it safe from the terrible old thin bag they were in. as it came open in her fingers and she reached in with no idea what it was I began to get her ready for this surprise. Her eyes were unable to comprehend what she was holding, so I began to explain the best I could. Her eyes came up to mine with question marks in the glare.

"I found these pieces of gold and in the bottom there are diamonds. Her eyes just bugged out. I knew she had a million questions so I tried to explain with passion in my heart to ask for time.

"I can see these are all uncut Glenda"? "Where and how did you get these?"

"It's a long story but I assure you they are mine as I found them and where I found them the people had never ever heard of Gold or Diamonds I can assure you in their time1438."

After a moment for her to get ahold of herself.,I began to slowly explain how this had all happened to me. And where I had been.and I wanted to know how long I had been gone.

She had been waiting for me for 2 months and a half. That was hard to believe because I spent some serious time traveling through time. I knew it would be hard for her to believe so I changed the subject to something I knew would hold her interest for a long time to come.

She kept touching my arm or my hand and tears were still falling. So I said please calm down and listen to me, "I found your Suit Of Armor Elaine!" She sat up straighter and blinked and started to ask me the questions I knew she wanted to ask.

Elaine spoke first, "I lost you on that busy street when you went into the Antique Store in front of me," and I told her I had heard her but I saw my Grandfather Clock and couldn't wait to get close, and then I called out your name and there was no one there but me and the Grandfather Clock" and all of a sudden I was alone.!

I walked outside a back door to get some air and kept calling your name but you were not there and I found a chair and sat down to get my breath.

So after that I went back inside but everything had changed, I did not know where I was anymore,so I returned to the porch and sat back down in the chair where I went to sleep again immediately. When I woke up I was not there anymore. I was in a field" I could see her eyes not wanting to believe me or hear anymore so I stopped.

Starting again I knew had her attention, when I put the Gold in her hands, while she rolled the gold and diamonds in her hands her face took on many expressions, her eyes roaming over me.

"Are you ready for me to tell you more"? She said "Ok I guess."

"It is hard to tell because I was in another time of the year, 1438 the first time, blinking her eyes she repeated "the year 1438?".

She saw the shocked look and knew that it was going to be a long time coming and trying to make her understand most likely would never happen either but I knew I had to try.

I saw the looks on her face, but what else was I going to do but try to explain this to her. I had thought the gold and diamonds would do it, raw and uncut straight out of the ground, but the more I talked the more questions she had. I had absolutely expected this but it was far more difficult than I thought.

"Elaine surely you knew that something bad had happened, when I disappeared from you, right?

I was lost. In the most uncertain times, more like stranded in another world. I know that you cannot imagine how horrible it was but it did happen, and I thank God I survived. Almost murdered, almost died from a sickness on the boat, tied up and thrown into bowls of this nasty disease ridden maggot filled boat. Where my only choice to survive was to murder the men when darkness fell and they were all drunk. I kept it together for a while then everything would change and I wound up in another time frame. I had to start all over again. Every morning when my eyes opened I prayed for you and that I would go back home, And you were waiting for me, because I had no idea if I ever would end up home again, or would I be alive or dead, and in another time. So my dreams and hopes and plans kept me sane.

Surely you can understand what I'm telling you, because it has been so bad for me, to be lost in time. No words or pictures could ever describe the turmoil in that lifetime.

But I had the brain to gather those diamonds and the gold and to hang on to it hoping one day I would get back to you. And most certainly this would be my only proof. In my mind over and over again I wished I had a camera. And then I woke up and was in the most strange of places I was on a ship and I was hiding in the bottom of my Grandfather Clock that was on this ship.

And it was enormous in size Elaine. It was so big I could have another person in there with me. I saw her eyes blinking. "I know this is a remarkable story but it is true Elaine, '' I begged, I promise, look at me, do I look like I was having fun or maybe hiding from you?"

"You look like a skeleton and I'm trying, but I really don't care. I just want you to know that God brought you back to me, back here with me, "Elaine listen,

I most certainly have lived through horrors you would never believe In another time? Yes, I realise that is not anything you can believe unless you have been there. But this is me and I don't lie and I do not make up things like this, how could I?"

"She was listening to me with horror on her face, but the happiness that I saw was still there.

Behind all her worry lines that were new to me because she certainly did not have them before.

I escaped the ship after a while and luck was there for me this time. I was running through the fields, looking back at every twenty steps to make sure they were not behind me, to get away from the pirates who murdered and killed people everywhere they went.

Then I saw this house and went running to it. The people there saw me running toward them with my arms up in the air, and thought I was Scotia, their daughter who had been captured by some pirates on the beach one day. I looked exactly like her, which I didn't believe until she returned one morning several months later, and then we were like twins. Thinking I had escaped they took my story as I had been trying to explain to them, and took me in, and I had to adapt to be able to eat and survive. This was the first time I went into another time, there are more things I had to live through but while I was there on that ship I saw your Suit Of Armor! It was the exact one we have been searching for and it is absolutely from another time."

I could see her expression changing from one look to another look, possibly not believing me at all. I knew it was going to be hard to get anyone to believe me but I had the jewels, and experiences only I know how to tell.

"Stop," she cried. "I don't want you to rehash this any more. You have been through enough." lowering her head I heard her thanking God for my appearance.

I could see her eyes and she continued to wring her hands, she looked like she was going to cry, "but I have you back, and I actually was running out of money a week ago, think about that, not funny, but true, so I called to transfer some more into my card,and I knew I was not leaving you behind, I knew something bad had to have happened and so I waited, and I went to the Antique Market daily and searched until dark every day,asking people questions, day after day, and some days I sat on the chairs in front of a cafe and searched the faces looking for you," then she broke and cried again. I was out of money but not hope, and the feeling that you were trying to get home to me kept me sane.

"I'm sure in the days to come your story will come full circle and I will listen to every word waiting for you to become real tome and I won't have to sit and search anymore for you, Elaine broke in,

"But now that we are calmed down, can you please tell me more about the Suit Of Armor you found, and just where did you find it?

"It Was also on that first Pirate Ship, the first few days I was not allowed to move from the corner they had thrown me into, but I got the feeling that I needed to try to get out and I started moving around more after a few days because they stopped watching me so closely. I kept thinking what are they worried about. I'm stuck here and can't get out or off this ship.and when I discovered I was beside the Grandfather Clock, that day I felt a chill go over my body, so I made the most of that time and after I found the Grandfather clock I explored more when they were busy, and I kept exploring the clock and the Armor daily for you.

For days I was so lonely and no one ever came to check on me, or saw me looking at the clock or the Suit of Armor, and it became my safe zone. I would sit next to it and the next day I would move to the clock. All the time watching the flurry of activity all around the ship. Trying to learn the activities and a possible escape.

. My heart hurt that I couldn't show it to you. Many times I broke down wishing I had a camera. But that was crazy considering where I was.

And always knowing that not one single person would ever believe me, if I survived the situation made it so much worse. There were days when I cried all day, and nights when I looked for a way off this horrible ship, but yet knowing that I had found what we were searching for for so long made it more impossible to have a plan to escape.

She was finally calming down, I saw my sister coming around and back to normal at last.

The happiness that flowed through my veins as I tried to settle back into my world was overflowing.

"The Suit Of Armor was in perfect condition. Like new. Who knew someday 500 years in the future someone would be able to see the real Armor?"

I told her, "There was red on it and it was bright."

I could see her smile touch the sides of her sad face at last. "The only photos we ever got to see were sketchy at best and always in black and white, but a lady told us several years ago, the history about this Suit Of Armor was real, but it was not proven, but the talk about it was supposedly accurate.. And just someone's memory had inspired those old drawings we had seen. We have seen those drawings and the color was what we couldn't decide. So you kept repeating there is red on it and in our minds it had to be red.

You, Elaine, were comparing it to a Suit we saw in the North of Scotland in Drummond Castle. Do you remember the day we first saw it? But then how could we ever forget that day, do you remember, the cold was hurting our face and the wind made it almost impossible to walk and not fall down at the same time. The temperature in Scotland is usually mild but in the far north of Scotland the ocean winds made it bitter, and some days it was hard to even stand up very long.

And after that we made yearly trips to the North of Scotland, and yes To the same area known as John-O'Groats, the story went that John had seven sons, and they did not get along at all and forced the man to build seven doors into his home, so each son had his own entrance, there for the fighting stopped. The story was amazing, you do remember it right?" "yes I do, it was almost like someone made it up but there it was and with seven doors and one front door.

"The Farthest Most Northern Point In all of Scotland" and the only thing we always found was that the two oceans, the Atlantic and the North Sea, still met and sprayed into the air, and it was still spraying. We both laughed at the moment we remembered that story."

I kept talking.

"You were still hoping to find your Suit of Armor, and I was still searching for the Clock, and finding even more information that could possibly lead us to it, was a great lure!Remember?"

When all of a sudden we went back the next year to John O Groats to see if what we had heard about was what we were searching for and no,it was not there. The owners supposedly had taken it to Thurso, and then we drove all that way, just to find it had been taken to London to be put on display. Oh I remember how upset you were. And I think we went to London soon after that, am I right" I asked, my memory was a bit fuzzy., and still we did not ever see it again."

Looking at her sister she had the feeling of everything coming together at last.

"So, here's what I think,"seeing the dreaded look on her face I continued,``should we give up, pack up, and buy new tickets for our trip home?" "What thoughts do you have now that I'm back?" reaching over to hold her lost sister in her arms was a good feeling, and she needed that feeling with her sister

She waited for a response.

Sitting cross legged on her chair, Elaine said she didn't want to go home yet. The surprise answer to the question that really had only one answer in her mind was not what she expected to hear,."Ok she said softly waiting to hear the regrets she thought would surely come next. "What are you talking about Elaine?"

Elaine shifted in her chair, crossed her legs and said "I don't want us to go home without trying one more day on the same street we found, with all those antiques!" the shocking words were echoing in her ears. "Finally I spoke up, "that was where all our trouble came from" I said in my most dreaded voice!

Elaine said she wanted some one on one time with me to try to make sure I was good. I was fine. But who knows how I might be in a day or two. It was not something I was too sure about at the moment, but I felt like I was fine.

To me It was as if some of these people did not want to believe what I had been through. But then I am the only one who knows all that has happened to me and I am not sure if they would ever believe me even with the gold staring them in the face.I knew all I had to do was pull out those shocking beautiful uncut diamonds, not to mention the gold nuggets that looked like rocks.but I was not ready to show them yet, even though I knew it would prove it. They were so unusually big, and in my mind only the rich and famous ever had the possibility of acquiring anything like these.

"I am tough as nails" I said with shock on my face.to which I replied without a thought,

Don't you think we should go home while everything is in our favor?"

I asked one last time.I saw her smile and I also knew we were heading down to the Antique district where all this had happened to me.

I asked for thirty minutes more to rest and to find a bite to eat before we went out and she agreed. I still did not know why she wanted to go back out.

After we had a snack in a corner bar we hailed a cabby and asked to be dropped off in the Antique District. While we rode through the streets I had a bad feeling that this could make things worse than ever but hoped for the best. Whenever I thought of all the things I had been through I had the chills. And to be home in 2020 was more than I could ever hope for.

After about twenty minutes we arrived where I remembered the blue door was.and it was not a place I had ever thought I would be again. While I was lost in time I had made myself promises that if I ever got home again I Antiquing was never to enter my mind again. I even prayed to God to save me and that all I wanted was to get home again safe.

Praying "Please God watch out for us because I'm not sure that we would ever survive those things again.

But here I was in the Cabby with Elaine, acting as if all those months were erased and I was there again where it all happened to me. When the Cabby pulled over I felt a shiver go down my arms and automatically I felt fear. I looked at my sister but she had a smile on her face. She said she was so glad to be out of that.

I tried to share her feelings but all I could feel was dread and fear. I kept it off my face for a long time and then as we rounded this corner I saw the Blue door. Chills raced over me. Fear jumped into my brain. I automatically reached out to protect my sister but she took my hand and assured me we were fine. To me that meant this is where this all started. And the Blue Door was sparkling off the sunlight. So I felt like the sun could not cause what had already happened to me again, and I kept walking. When we approached the Blue Door Elaine said ``this is where you saw the Clock and maybe you have led me to the Armor"!

I walked behind her and let her reach out for the door knob, and as soon as she touched it she jerked away. Then the Door swung open and the cold air came out to blast us in the face. Elaine turned around and grabbed my hand and said, ``Come on, we are fine.'' but I knew we were not!

It was dark and cool and I remembered it all the way it had been, because it was the first time I came in here.

CHAPTER 30

The lighting was so bad. It was almost dark as night. In there. I followed Elaine keeping close enough but staying behind. All at once she turned and pointed to the right. It was exactly as I had seen it the first time we entered this building. I stopped and stood still, looking left and right but I did not see the door I had gone out into the first time I was here. I had a forbidding feeling that kept saying turn around and fo out. Elaine kept pulling me toward the back of the dark room. "Was it this dark before?" "Yes, maybe even darker than before.

Elaine was not at the least frightened and I knew she thought the Armor might be in there and she would find it if it was. There was no doubt at all what was going on in her mind. She didn't believe me or she would not have come back here at all.

It hurt me that she didn't believe me and I had nothing to prove it with but my jewels. There was no way she could not believe them. She held them in her hands for pete's sake!

And then there it was, right in front of me. The Grandfather Clock. Just as it was on the ship. Only in perfect condition.

We stood back and could not believe our luck today. Behind us, there they were, two old nasty dirty stuffed arm chairs, the sameones I had fallen into that day.. We backed up, right into them and both of us fell backward at the same time landing in the chairs and the smell was horrible, something you could not describe. And now it was on us. We sat still for a few minutes and then I saw the Clock in all its beauty, right in front of us. We were both silent at first and then we tried to get out of the chairs but it felt like we were stuck. I wiggle and she tried to stand up but we were stuck in them as tight as we could be. I remember we both looked back and forth but there was not a single person there but us. Then we both tried screaming, and kicking our feet to make noise and maybe attract somebody and get help. But nothing happened.

When we tried to rock the chairs we both fell backwards into a strange smoke filled area. Still stuck in the chairs we tried calling out. We tried to get up but we were stuck like glue. Elaine screamed out "I am stuck in this chair help me get out. But as I tried to move I was also stuck in this chair, and I had bad feelings that we were not where we should have been and then,it hit me, what if it has come to take me back again. I knew it was her idea but how stupid was I for following her.

Earlie in our hotel room, I remember asking Elaine and watching her expressions, to check if she thought it was safe for us to try this again. Especially after what had happened to me before.

I wondered as I sat there stuck like glue did she really believe me ever? And what about the gold and diamonds! We had purchased a glittery silver and ping plastic case in the hotel gift shop that was built well and heavy duty for the gold and diamonds and immediately took them to the bank, which just happened to be next door to the hotel she had been staying in. To open it we picked a combination that only the two of us would know. Our mothers birthday. Which was July 261921.

So now we knew they were safe, and we were not,but what if we never got back?

Then I asked her about where we were and what she thought now! I had a dreadful feeling that kept getting stronger as we moved about the darkly lit room.My heart was beating so hard, my hands were sweating and itching at the same time, with my brain saying ohhh noooo not again. and I felt a fear like we should not be here.

Cautiously searching my surroundings everything seemed to be similar to where we were when I found that snarky antique that took me away.

Waiting for her response which was not forthcoming right this minute, made me scared, because she did not answer me. And then there was a smoky thick feeling in the air. And we both had to be breathing it in, and then remembering the fear that I had brought with me, a fear that had been with me since I returned home to her, but it was here again. I felt my heart beating out of rhythm and knew we were in a different time. Since I had done this before several times my mind freaked out, and I seemed to hear myself screaming,

I guess we were asleep because when we woke up or whatever had happened we were not in the Antique Store. Then I felt Elaine tugging on my sweater sleeve with a frantic pulling sensation

Trying to get my bearings I leaned over to stand up but she pulled me down and we both landed on the floor of some old nasty building. We reached out and together we tried to stand up but for some weird feeling I had in my brain I knew we were on a ship!"

Oh dear God" was all I could think because it felt like when I had been on the pirate ship the first time. Looking around the darkness overwhelmed us both and we saw nothing, but we felt the water hitting the Ship and I knew.

I felt her grabbing my sleeve and I heard her crying. "I'm so sorry that I pulled us both into this mess" she was crying. And while I was trying to comfort her the ship came to a standstill. Within a few seconds we heard all kinds of screening and we could smell smoke, and then we felt something hit the side of the ship.

I took Elaine hands in mine and I said in honesty that it felt like before when I was captured, telling her to keep quiet so not to have anyone come down to find us, it made me wonder if we just suddenly appeared here from the Antique Shop. and was that how I ended up there the first time?

My mind was spinning in ten different directions as I tried to come up with a plan of escape, knowing full well that wherever we ended up it was going to be a nightmare from hell. And the worst part was Elaine would never believe it. In time as I did it all came to be true. I asked her to hide behind these big barrels in the back until I came back down, explaining that I had to see if land was near, and not to make a sound. She was shaking and absolutely did not hear anything I had said. So I shook her lightly and pushed her into the corner and covered her with a dirty old tarp so no one would see her. She didn't move or say a thing.

As I sneaked up the rickety ladder that had more rungs gone than any ladder I had ever seen before, I hid well and I saw things I had seen before. I was stunned but it even looked like the first ship I was on. My heart was beating so fast that when the ship stopped moving and I heard them running all over the ship, I almost fainted. Thinking how this could be happening again. Then I shut my eyes for two minutes and I began to make a plan. Sneaking down the ladder I crawled over to where Elaine was hiding. Pulling the tarp off of her I said in quiet words that only she could hear, we have to jump over the side and swim to shore now. Up on top they had eaten and it looked like the men were all sleeping. Now is our time to leave.

"But we cant jump off her in the middle of the ocean.. she said to me with fear in her voice. So I said the first thing that came to my mind, "it's not too far to the shore. And if this makes you feel any better I almost think this is where I landed the first time, and "reaching to stroke her hair trying anything I could to calm her down "if im right Im taking you see Scotia in flesh and blood." her eyes wandered around this dirty area where we had been for a couple of days and she said "lets go, I won't make a sound, I promise, just get us off this thing called a ship. It seems to me like it should be a junk yard somewhere ready to burn."I knew some of what she was feeling because not too long ago this was me and I had made it back.thinking about my experience gave me clues and told me what to say to my sister to calm her down and Now I was in control.

I took her hand and we both crawled up the ladder and I was right there was not one person in sight because they were all drunk and out cold. That makes it better I told her as we crawled to the side of the ship and lowered our self down into the water.

Quiet as a mouse.

Once I thought I heard someone yelling, and I prayed they were not yelling because they saw us.

But we were out of sight and they were all drunk we guessed.

Quietly we moved in the water straight to the shore. Once we got our legs back we started to walk as quickly as we could. We kept looking back but they were not aware we were gone so luck was on our side.

After about an hour of walking we sat down and we both said I'm hungry at the same time. Smiling at my bewildered sister but knowing how I had felt when this happened to me I tried to compensate and help her adapt, because as I told her Scotia and my other family were here somewhere. So we walked and walked and walked some more. When we were so tired we both sat down and couldn't move a leg.

Later on, after we had rested a while, I saw a stream off to my right, and as I stood up so I could see better, Elaine said ``what are you doing?''

I said you won't believe this but this is the stream where Scotia and I found the Gold and not far from here the diamonds, please sit down I'm not going to leave you, I promise.

I had wanted to run, but I was not going to leave her here in this nowhere, we were stranded in, but I DID know where we were, so first thing I had to do was calm my sister, who thought I was leaving her,I guess, and as Elaine screamed stop, what is wrong? I went to her side to tell her why I was so excited. "Surely you haven't forgotten the gold and diamonds in the bank where we took them have you?". Elaine had calmed down and I knew exactly what she was feeling because it had not been long that I was in this same place lost as she was now.

"Do you remember where they lived, or how to get back there?" she asked me, and then I saw she was getting tired, and I was tired too but we needed to find them. And what if this was not the same place I jumped off that boat and I'm running the wrong way. We walked and talked and then out of the corner of my eye I saw the running water where we had washed our clothes for her Mother. I screamed with joy now because, before I saw this it was the blind leading the blind, only she didn't know it. She was trusting,me and I only had glimpses of that time with her.

The only thing that made me happy was the fact that Scotia and my other family were close by, and this was something that had never entered my mind..I needed to sit down when the time was right, and try to explain to Elaine the people who took me in and the experience of trying to fit in with a family five hundred years in the past.

All I had to do was sort out the path to get to them again..remembering exactly how I would get to them was harder than I had thought it was going to be. I can't even think how wonderful it will be to see them again. Seeing the family who took me in and treated me as their Scotia. This was never anything I had ever imagined doing again.

And then Elaine will begin to believe me.was what I kept telling myself day after day. I had really loved them and they loved me too. Even now I could picture them sitting at that old rough table and chairs that were rougher even.

Elaine had to keep in front of me after I explained this was the right way. We were walking very slowly now as we were so tired. Off to my left I saw a stream and told Elaine we needed to go get some drinking water because I was so thirsty. She responded "so am I but will it be safe?" "yes I drank that water the whole time I was here and believe me this water tastes like none you have ever tasted before. No chlorine, just fresh clean water. I saw Elaine lean down and get a handful of water. I knew soon we would be close to Scotia's home so we slowed down a bit. I was watching Elaine drink her fill of water when she turned around and screamed "run sister something is in the water, like the gold that you brought home with you".

That could only mean we are closer than I thought we were. It had been only a little while ago since I was here but it felt like forever. Running down to the water there she was picking up gold rocks just like I did when I first saw them.

I knew It was so exciting to her, and then I had to remind her that we had no idea how long we might be here and where we could keep them, because they were so heavy.

"And what if a thief came upon us "? she asked with her big brown eyes clearly intoxicated with the touch of so much gold.

"Need I remind you we are not home and these people don't even have a clue what this is, let alone the value in our world".She smiled the sister smile I used to keep in my mind when I was lost here with no one but these people who took me in and actually loved me.

"I kept you in my mind while I was lost because your memory kept telling me that, if this was not a dream, then surely it was a nightmare and I'd wake up. It was hard to explain so I felt like Elaine would have to meet them, and then make her own decision about the future with them, while we had no idea how to reverse the time frame and go home again.

At least we were not put in some other time frame trying to make the days go by with no ideas to lead us or to help us accept this mess.

We sat down on the bank and drank more water and when Elaine asked me about the ship, was this the one where I had to kill the Pirates to take the ship to a better port to find a way home.?

Answering her truthfully I said yes it was.

But it was something that had to be done and I did it with the boy who was on board, and I even thought many times about what if I had killed him?

He had to have been asleep that night or he would have picked up those metal cups I found and had a drink himself..He was my lifesaver. I had saved his life when I took the piece of long splintered wood out of his body and then I confessed that I had put the poison in that bottle and a drop in all of the cups when they were sleeping throughout the night.

Would things have turned out the way they did? She was worried about me having bad memories, and I reminded her that these people had actually loved me and begged me not to go.I even tried to pretend Scotia was you for a long time. Then one day she was my sister in this new period of time I had somehow landed in. It took me a while to accept them but they took to me immediately.

All these people and even my grandfather cried when I walked away that day.

Imagine that!

I really had been accepted and loved and from the very beginning, when they first saw me running up the hill towards their home.

With the Pirates chasing me it was truly a miracle that this turned out the way it did, imagine perfect strangers accepted me. Even though I looked like Scotia it took them no time at all to realise I was not her. The real Scotia had been kidnapped but she also returned.

That day I walked away from the sure thing, into a hopeful thing, and did not ever think I would ever see them again because I hoped I would be in another century and with my real family. The proof is there now, in both our minds.

So now we both know that the building we walked into yesterday, if it was actually haunted, then that is why we are here. But at night I really wondered, through all those days alone how I got there and how I would get back.

And now we are both here because there is something really bad in that shop. As much antiquing as we both do and have done here before you would think we would have heard stories about the Blue Door. but not a story one.

Actually the Blue Door should have told us something was wrong when we touched it the first time and it shocked us both, me more than you the first time I was lost, and then this time we actually somehow both ended up back in that shop. Knowing that was where the trouble came from I just can't understand what made you want to go back there. Even though we have done many sketchy things I think it was tempting fate in the face. I was ready to go home Elaine but no you just have one more hunt for the SUit Of Armor and I told you I saw it but it was not in this century and it made sense that we would never get the chance to find your dream or mine.

I have terrible memories of being in that clock "Is there no way you can remember that size?" She asked me.

I only know it was big enough to hold both of us captive for a long time with not one person ever thinking about looking inside it. It was very tall, maybe it was way, way, before they started dating things, and I can only imagine... Just think, Elaine there it was and I was inside it hiding for my life.

And then I saw the Suit of Armor, with the red on it. You were totally right about that, but how did you know the red paint or whatever it was, was on it? It broke my heart over and over again just to think about the chances that you would never be able to see it.

Elaine said "Ok enough about what I may or may not see, you still don't understand that, that was why I wanted to leave the hotel room and take you with me, one mire time, we could do this last time in London. Thinking we might never be able to do this again almost broke my heart, but knowing what you had been through I just knew you would never go Antiquing with any one ever again.

So, YES you are right.! This is all my fault. And even though I'm sorry I talked you into coming out with me, I never had bad thoughts about anything, but here are and how? Please tell me! And so now since you are the virtual time traveler "please get us back "!

Both of us were so unnerved but I knew Elaine was in a bad way. And I also knew there was not one thing I could do at the moment. "How did this happen? I heard her crying into her hands, and I went over and said "just stop ``. Elaine looked up and said you are right, and now it looks like we have traveled back in time again? But this time we are together!" We both managed a fake smile and then I hugged her for support, because I remembered when this first happened to me, and I had no one, and I made sure she knew she had me. And laughingly I said "yes and I am very experienced in time travel by now."! We both tried to laugh, but it didn't work this time at all.

So I had no one to lean on and then with my best smile beaming, I took her arm and told her I had murdered all those Pirates! This was my way to get her talking and I hoped it would work.

At first she looked alarmed then she sat down and shook herself and my sister was back. Not one time did she ask me to tell her what I had done to those Pirates. I thought that was a good thing.

I wasn't too sure I could explain why I did it so she would understand. Better to leave that alone. I was still trying to get it out of my mind even now.

Changing the subject totally I took her hand and we started to walk again. Leaving the stream behind I remembered that we saw more gold. And that had to mean we were actually not too far from Scotia and her family.

Thinking back I wondered how much time had gone by since I was rescued and came home. Would they remember me? Was the thing that came to my mind almost every day since we touched the door knob on the Blue Door. That evening as dark started to cover the land, and made everything harder for us who were already lost, I saw faint lights ahead of us.With no electricity We knew the dark would make things more difficult for us. Telling her" I remember Scotia's Mom lit those lights before dark would descend on the home. With a fire in the rooms it was always light enough for anyone to see the house before you really got there.

"Look Elaine" I pointed ahead to the dim lights. Where are they coming from" she asked me.

"I Am almost sure that is where we are headed. And If it is there will be 4 dogs barking before long, bringing the people outside to see what the commotion is about.

I was right, within five minutes the dogs began their protection mode, and barked like crazy wild animals

Since we had no lights they could not see us until we got closer. Then I heard the first familiar voice "Who is there?" It was my grandfather.

I called out loudly and he came running, and I told them I had returned to visit my family, and I called out his name. All at once the door burst open and people came rushing to us. Scotia was in tears, crying "how did you do it? how did you find your way back to us?" After all the hugs I turned to Elaine and said this is my sister, do you remember when I would tell you about her and how much I missed her?" Scotia finally let go of me, and went to meet Elaine. They were taken with each other immediately. When the Grandfather finally got to us we were almost to the house, and I saw the tears. I think I did not realise how much of an impact I had had on him when I was there. Elaine had been quiet but by the time we got in the house she had met them all and was in shock that I had actually gotten them back there. We all walked into the home that I had spent much time in and it looked the same as it did the day I said goodbye to all of them. Bringing with it many memories, all of them happy.

We were both very hungry so I asked if they might have a piece of bread they would share with us.

Almost at once they pulled out a chair for Elaine and I and we were seated around the fire.

Telling them how long it had taken her to find them again, the conversation flowed.

And no one asked about how they got there so she had no worries about the explanation. Grandfather sat down by me and said he had had many thoughts and worries about where I was a and if I was alright. When Scotia finally let go of me, we sat close together in a warm part of the home. Talking about things they had done and how much she had been missed.

This was the best surprise for the whole family in many years. Elaine seemed to be impressed by the family.

As it was late they were trying to make decisions as to where we would sleep. And Scotia spoke up and asked Elaine if she could sleep with them in her bed? ' Elaine looked my way and I shook my head yes, so it was settled. The night was dark but they had enough lights in the windows to make the home feel comfortable.

Grandfather came to hug her one more time and said that he had never thought he would see her again, and could not explain how he had missed her when she walked away that morning.. Because she had told them all the story about how she got there the first time, from running from the pirates, when they mistook her for their Scotia, the home felt comfortable to them that evening. Before long they went to bed. Grandfather had wanted to give her his bed again but she would not hear it, together they found blankets and slept on the floor. Elaine was in shock, but she felt the love they had for her sister, and then she knew the stories she had heard were even better now that she had arrived at this time and at this home.Sleep came fast and easy. The two were so tired, and Scotia just wanted to lay by her sister again.

"Tomorrow we will explain why I called her my sister, ''Scotia told Elaine, who couldn't wait to hear it from their point of view.

The last thing Scotia talked about before they were all asleep were the clear stones, and the Gold she had found with her. And wanted to hear what she had done with them. And another thing she wanted to know was how long she had been back home,in years and days, and how she got back there. And she wanted to know what ELaine thought about the stories she knew I had told her.

Tomorrow will be an exciting day, I thought right before I fell asleep, but not before I hoped it was not a wash day. She knew she would never forget those days.

The best thing had been finding Diamonds and Gold and the fact that no one even knew what it was, made it even more exciting.

Sleep came quickly for us, even being three in the bed, did not keep us awake. Scotia had her arms around me all night. The memories came back of the wonderful, olf fashioned times I had had here, and I did not hear a thing until the mother got up, and started the cooking. It all came back to me, and the smells and family I had left behind, made me smile.

As the time before Grandfather came and nudged them to wake them and when they were awake the smell of food was everywhere. I turned over to Elaine and I said you have never had any food like this before and I remember it took me a long time to get used to it. The bread is the only thing that kept me alive, until one day I asked to show them how we made Chicken and dumplings, of course using her biscuit dough made it easy. Her Mom boiled the chicken and you know the rest. Elaine smiled and wanted to go back to sleep but I told her, here they dont sleep much,. they were used to getting up literally with the chickens. It only took the sun five minutes shining into the windows,until we were all up, but with this being a new experience for Elaine she took to the schedule they imposed upon us as easily as I had before. Elaine relly asked a lot of questions, but the one that shook her was that no one in this house knew what the date was.She took me out on the porch and said "how do they not know what the date is' '?I already knew that but I just said that they were like in their own time and maybe their time did matter to them as much as it did in our time. Elaine and I were sitting on the porch while Mother cooked Breakfast. "What do you think I Asked my sister?"

We were in the oldest broken chairs I had ever seen in my life. But to them they were perfect. I told Elaine that and she said how did I go about asking them? so I answered "one day not long after they had taken me in as their daughter I fell through the chair I was sitting in, and when I hit the floor they came running to see if I was ok. I assured them I was, and offered to take it to the back where they burn the garbage in their time. But I was stopped and told they were going to fix it and they never threw away anything. That same chair probably belonged to Adam And Eve. I had joked and they just looked at me and said why were you laughing. Please tell us who Adam and Eve are, and maybe you have one of those things Scotia and you call it a photo?

After that I watched my words and became able to live a simple life like nothing you have ever even read about. You will see.

Elaine said, ``Is that a promise or a threat?" I replied "you will see. And you won't even be bothered after a while. But then we might get home soon so we always have that to look forward to...

She did not look as happy as I felt. Today I had to help her adapt as I had to. The food was smelling gross but Elaine never said a word. I on the other hand remembered the naasty food that at first I would say no thank you to, then as I grew weak and hungry I tried tasting and it really helped me a lot. I did eat it after all. And each day here was the same: up early to sleep in the dark, cut wood and carry it in and or stack it for the winter which I was told was bad here. And it was near us they said, like a season was a person. There were many things I learned, and their winter was terrible. Snow abounded everywhere, but temperatures most of the time felt like maybe 15 to 30 degrees, but remember I was only guessing. But when spring arrived it went smooth just like at home in Wisconsin beautiful days long days and it felt like maybe eighty in the days. You have no idea how hard it was to adjust here. It took me a long time, but I adored all the people, and the Grandfather was the best ever.

A few days later after we had helped with all the chores, Scotia asked me about the rocks I had taken home, and if I wanted to go get more. Elaine looked at me and we both answered together, yes.

Scotia wanted to know what we had done with them, so when Elaine looked at me, and I saw it in her eyes, I let her take the floor. "Oh Scotia you wouldn't believe what we did with them, there is a store at home that took them and made necklaces for us. '' They were all staring so I figured we had said something they might not understand, and I reached under my shirt and held the necklace up to show Scotia. She was amazed in my words, and then she walked over to touch them, "his is so beautiful," she said. Then she told us she had never seen anything like it before. I asked her if her mother had a wedding ring, or necklace?" it was as if she did not know what I was talking about. She had a look on her face that told us she had not seen anything like that before. With that said we changed the subject.

Elaine and I went out on the broken down porch,which had happened in the time since I was there. And we sat on the steps. Enjoying the Sunshine. We both wanted to know when this was going to end but how did we know? We just didn't.

There was a lot of noise in the house and so we stood up and went inside, the mother was getting buckets together for us to get water. That made me think maybe we should go to the creek where I had seen the gold nuggets. Scotia mentioned it first, "how would you like to take some meat and we will go get you some more gold rocks"? I remember that you really liked them, and can you tell me what you have done with them. I seem to remember that you said they were worth money, and remember I did not know what money was but you described it to me as a barter thing. Did you trade them for food or clothing? I'm not sure what you would have done in your time when you described to me what jewelry was. Do you have any new jewelry this time?"

We both just shook our heads but then mentioned finding more and she was up and ready, telling her mother where we were going we took off and walked a long way. I didn't remember it being so far away.

Scotia's Mother gave us food in a bucket that looked like it came from Jesus when he was here.

The mother waved goodbye and off we went. It had been about three days since I had anything good to eat, and I was so hungry my stomach was growling. Scotia looked at me and asked if we needed food? "No I'm fine I just wish we had an egg sandwich to take with us, because I remember that it was a pretty good walk and carrying buckets of clothing was hard on us."

"Oh today my mother said we did not need to do any washing, and she made us some food, which I have in the bucket. I smiled at that and so did Elaine. We both were so hungry. We had not gotten used to her food yet, but I remembered that I did finally eat and got full after a while. So I encouraged Elaine to take a few bites at a time so we did not get sick. It was odd but there was not anything there that we could cook for them. Meaning they had no food like we knew. Reminding her there was no Dr, and no medicine. Only what we could see. That was their life. It was so sad to see them work so hard and have so little. But their life was full and they were all happy. Not knowing was better than knowing and not being able to have it, in my way of thinking.

Each one of us had a bucket and as we walked Elaine asked minimal questions, just anything that we could talk about.

Time passed and I was getting tired when Scotia said, look girls it's right there. And she was at the same spot I remembered. "Elaine take off your shoes and let's get in there, because that is when I found them, when my feet started to hurt. They were sharp and shiny.

So here we were, and in only a few seconds I heard Elaine say look over here, and we both went over to her spot, and she had pieces of gold the size of a nichol. She was so excited and I had found a lot of little slivers, so I showed her mine.

CHAPTER 31

After about an hour we were sitting on the bank just delirious with our finds. I could tell Scotia had no idea why we were so excited, so Elaine had made up a story, and started to tell her. She was amazed at the ridiculous story, but she did laugh.

"My turn," I said, and I started to tell her about the little bears and Goldilocks.

Scotia never moved, thoroughly amazed with my story, and at the end we laughed so hard she almost fell off the bank into the knee deep water. That would have been bad, because the number one thing we did not have was a change of clothes.

Looking at the sun as it was going down, we got up and started to head back to her home, when we picked up the buckets full of gold we realised they were too heavy and we all three had to start putting it back in the creek. I smiled at Elaine and she said this almost makes me want to cry, and laugh at the same time. "Who will ever believe us?" she asked me. Scotia had asked us what we would do with them. We were both dumbfounded. Thinking hard Elaine and I both opened our mouth at the same time

"It is for adornment in the church Parrish," I first said, quickly realising I knew nothing about any Paris. I felt proud to have come up with this answer, and then my sister said we can make jewelry with gold. `We both saw the look on her face but there was no other way to describe it to her so she would understand, first of all they did not have money at this time. Here it was strictly barter for things, and the gold could have been decoration for the Church.

Offerings had only really been used in the Church but they did not have a church, she told us. I even remember asking one night when we were just talking about how they bought things. Asking what they used to pay for things. Again a stumbling block because it seems like they did not have anything they could not make or build or even kill to eat.

Sitting down thinking about that when we were waiting to eat, I was amazed at the simple life these people lived and they were all happy as they could be with their life. As I had been when I was here.it jhad taken a toll at first but I grew to love them and they had also returned the love to me.

The walk back took us through some beautiful scenery, and the day was just too perfect, but it took longer than we thought, and with all that gold that was so heavy, we stumbled a lot and when with an eager look on her face Scotia said "why don't you just throw some of those bigger away, I can tell they are so heavy. I can see the strain is heavy on you.

Both of us looked at her with the same thoughts, like oh no you wont need to help us, and thinking that she had no idea that we were thinking about the dollars we would get when we got home, we pretended they were not so heavy at all.

Again she commented on our strained faces.

She asked us why we wanted to carry all those back to her home, mentioning again that there was nothing that we could do with it. And she said let me help you with the heavy load you are keeping.

"And then I can help share the load, just put some in my basket here. "Pointing to her small basket with some plants in it."

"Oh, thanks for offering but, no we won't throw it away, and we can't take your kindness for granted. We are fine'.

The walk was harder than we thought but we really did want to bring them back, hoping in our minds that if we got the break and found a way to go back we would have this to prove what we had said, and it was worth the work of keeping it with us at all times for right now.

Changing the subject slowly my sister asked me about the glass rocks we had found brefor. Scotia looked at me and I told her Elaine we were washing clothes one day and standing in the water the rocks were sharp and when we picked up a few I had loved them and then we had gathered them because I wanted to take them when and if I found a way to go home again.

Scotia asked us if we wanted to go back on our way home?

Looking at Elaine, I saw the excitement in her eyes, so I spoke up first saying that these gold rocks were probably all we could carry today. She nodded but then Scotia said that we were so close, why not lay these gold ones down and cross this stream over to one more stream that was not far and we could show her how beautiful they were. Then she commented "let me tell you the clear ones are much prettier than those old yellow ones."Elaine and I looked at each other and inside we were laughing at her words "old dirty yellow ones". I said yes but lets go home now with these and save the others for another day lease?" Scotia smiled her beautiful smile and we headed back to our new home.

That night after we helped Scotia's Mom do her dinner, which Elaine had not gotten used to at all yet, her Mom sent us out of her cooking room which she called it, and we went outside to the porch to enjoy the evening breeze, where Elaine told me how hungry she was for the first time.

Watching Elaine look out to who knows where I remembered how lost I had felt the first few long days after I had turned up there, and understanding the feeling, but not really able to help her cope, was hard for me to watch.

Thinking about it I remembered that I had gone through a lot of terrible things before I wound up here with Scotia and her family.

And then one day the real Scotia had come back home and they all understood my many questions when I first found them.

I did handle this better than Elaine because I had been there before.So while I was sitting on the porch I tried to think about our next move. There was not really any kind of plan but in time we would maybe wake up back home? That's just a dream I told myself smiling.

Then we both went into the house and found our blankets and curled up in the corner where we had been sleeping. We both had reconciled ourselves to the fact, that for now this was home.

The sun came shining in but the wind was colder than I remember from before when I had run off that Pirates ship, hoping no one was chasing after me and never looking back until I saw that house I was heading towards. The fact that they thought I was Scotia made it easier for me.

Elaine had to adjust but she had me there to try and keep her head up. So far it has worked well enough I was guessing.

All these people were so kind to her, and I knew she had fears that she had not told me about but every day she seemed to be accepting that we were there and there was nothing we could do about it.

Walking up behind her I at first thought she was crying, then I asked her if everything was alright, and she said yes she supposed it was.

Turning around she touched my arm and said 'how long do you think we will stay here?' of course there was no answer but I had been thinking about this also in the past few days. I knew it must be taking its toll on her.

"There is one thing I can think of that might take us away from here but it is only a chance. We could end up in worse places so do you want to hear my thoughts or not?".

Her face had a tiny smile on it and was the first encouraging thing I had seen in many weeks.

I knew in my heart that she might be acting like she was ok, but I knew she was still torn apart at the fact that she was here. It made good logic for her to know it's a true story, and the ending bringing me back home must be hammering in her brain.

She had said many times that all this was her fault. And I always said there was no way we could have known this would happen to me again.but it was her idea to return one more time and we did.

And now we are going through the motions of being normal.

Always knowing this was not normal. Nor was it an accident. We both simply tempted fate, and the old saying "once burned you learned" was not true for her but only me.

It had happened to me and God brought me through some terrible things, just to do it again. No it was both our faults and now we were learning a second valuable lesson!

Neither one of us would tempt fate again, and all we wanted was to go home.

She had adjusted to the time and to the people she had needed for our survival, but even though I did see affection in her eyes all the time now, I knew it wasn't enough, because she was not the same person at all.

I knew she was very afraid, and I was afraid to tell her my thoughts. I wanted her to feel like I thought she was good with everything that had happened to us so far. And I knew there was more to come, for her to understand and deal with.but she didn't.

I told her,"Ok listen and tell me what you think about my plan,"she seemed to brighten up a little with the thought that I had a plan,but the fear was still there, so obvious to me.

"I lived it, I saw it, and I felt it", so I did know how she felt but there was only a plan in my mind.

We can travel down the river to the the opening of the Ocean and follow it until we find a ship or vessel that we might be able to get ourselves on, and offer ourselves as people who could help them hunt, or control the boat while they hunt for food, in exchange for passage to the next large port, or village, or even until we can find a larger ship that we can get on as workers, for passage.

Listening to me she thought about it for a minute then said "please tell me how you got back to our time and home".

I was sure that when I found that boat, that eventually took me home, after all the horrible things that happened along the way, and the men allowed me on and made me work, I was pretty sure we would never get that lucky again and so even though I was afraid, it was worth taking the chance and I talked her into leaving Scotia and her family, by telling her we needed to move on and then no matter what direction we headed, maybe we would get lucky, it was a big chance but I knew we didn't have any chance staying there any longer than we had. I explained all we had was hope and luck to depend on.Late that night I talked about how I had gotten on that ship later, when I was returned home, out of shock, surrounded by another time I woke up and found myself home. And all we could hope for was that same chance and that same luck to wake up one morning and be home again. I saw desperation in her eyes.

Sitting down beside her she took my hand and said she knew it was her fault that this happened to us, because she had wanted one more chance to find her antique Armor, never thinking that we might be swept back in the past again. And she was so sorry.and she knew that we neither one knew how to get back and we should just go day by day and every morning when we woke up we should be happy to be alive, and that through teamwork we would put our minds to it and in the end we would find a way to get home. Begging me for forgiveness, I had to laugh!

Telling her there was nothing to forgive but a lot of things for us both to understand and putting it in motion was our project moving forward.

The very next evening I asked Scotia to sit down with us and we wanted to tell her something. I immediately saw something shiver in her eyes.

I knew she knew we were planning to leave. We spent a lot of time that evening talking to her and letting her know how much we loved our new family but that it was time for us to go.

"Where will you go"? She asked in a sad voice "I don't want to miss you again and your sister has grown to love us too"! She exclaimed. Turning her face sideways to wipe the tears away. The sadness was clearly in her voice when she asked,

"Why can't you just stay here?" you are so loved here and now we love two of you, you feel like a part of our family", I felt her pain, she was begging.

Looking back and forth the three of us knew the time had come.

"I know we will miss you every bit as much as you will miss us, Scotia" Just saying her name sent a chill rushing through my heart. We had a lot of memories before but this time it is more than memories, it was our hearts, and they were breaking.

Turning my head I wiped my eyes with my sleeve, pausing a second I looked at Elaine, and I saw her tears too, and it flashed through my mind how I would love to have a kleenex to wipe my eyes.

There was a moment and we got it together and went inside to tell Scotia's Mom.

Elaine laid her head on my shoulder and said softly, so only I would hear, "I feel like I'm losing my family too."

The time had come. When we all sat down to eat, Scotia told them our plan. There was a lot of crying, and we all knew it had come to an end. "I told them how much I had gone through, after I left them, but in the end I went home again. So we do not have a clue as to when or where, but we would go.

"I just wish I could show you the world we live in so you would be happy for us, but we can't, so in the morning after we eat we will head out, on the same path I chose that day so long ago".

As you can imagine we will be going home. So please no more tears. I looked at Elaine and said, "if only we had a polaroid for memories." Again I saw their eyes as they had no idea what a polaroid was.

It seemed to have been accepted, and we went to our room to sleep our last night here with these beautiful people who made a tremendous effect on our lives.

I smelled the meat that was cooking. Elaine was awake and we both were so sad that it was hard to talk. We got dressed and rolled up our blanket that we had been using since we arrived, and we put the gold in their box on the floor. I said who knows maybe someday in their life gold will become valuable even to them. But Elaine shook hre head and said,"I don't think so, and when they find it they just take it outside, throw it away. Her eyes were sad.

CHAPTER 32

After breakfast and some hugs we walked out the door and kept walking, never looking back because we were both afraid and had no idea where this day would lead us. I did not want to see their sad faces again. This was the best way.

After about an hour I told Elaine that we were close to the Ocean and walked a little faster and in no time at all we could smell the salt water.

Knowing we were close, I was hoping there might be a ship somewhere. I had explained to Elaine that we had no choice but to hide on any ship that we would come upon. She did not agree, because after hearing my stories she had new fears everyday, but she went on with my plan.

It was getting dark, and I said we needed to find a place secure enough to get thru the night, so I saw the perfect place not two hundred feet from where we were standing, we found a tree that had fallen and had all kinds of debris around the base, the base was huge enough for both of us to climb in and not be too uncomfortable, so we climbed in and moved a barrier to hide us tonight from any animals or even any people that might be near.

All through the long chilly night, jumping when there was a sound that sounded too close to us,we huddled close together, feeling safe, as we waited for the sun to come up, and finally when we did fall asleep we were not cold or wet, just comfortable enough to finally fall asleep and get the first real real rest we had had in quite a few days..

Waking to the sunshine in our face's and then having to readjust to realizing where we were, we quickly got up, and took off walking towards where we thought the ocean might be. We could smell the salt water so we knew it had to be close.

I had told her about my journey and the murders, and the escape. I saw fright on her face. "I'm not saying this might happen but the bottom line is we will have to go where we can find escape to some place that would be to our benefit.

"This doesn't mean things will happen that way again, but if we could get on and hide we could put miles between where we were now.

We walked all day. We both mentioned at one time or another how beautiful and serene this time was compared to our time. Not without thinking "how could this be real" we kept on.

Never hearing a sound and never getting close to the ocean, was so hard to believe.. When the sun was overhead we searched for and found some black berries in a bush and ate them to fill our hunger. Then we went down to the gurgling stream we had listened to all night, and got water. We were so thirsty that we did not even remember the last time we had water. After that we walked some more.

After an hour or more, who could tell without a watch, I said let's take five minutes. Ok She said, "My feet hurt," Elaine said as she sat down to rub them. "Mine do too. I showed her the scratches and cuts, and we compared our painful feet.

"What I wouldn't give for my Nikes!" I said. For the past few days we had been through a lot and I worried about my sister. I felt like it was my fault. All of this. But we had to move on. I always remembered that I got home before and we would get home too.

I really saw her fear that was still there. I asked her "Are you ok?" She smiled and said "this is not the time or place to be complaining and I still do not believe where we are. Oh and by the way where on earth are we?

I had to laugh at that question. She said, "I will keep my hopes up that maybe you do know. But I see you don't know at all." Both of us had to laugh at that remark.

"Come on", I held out my hand. And we were off again. Going nowhere, but knowing we had tofind water and get some bearings then, if we were lucky.

We must have walked for quite a few miles when we saw an opening in a hillside. "A cave"I said pointing to it. I saw Elaine smile. Then we inched closer so as not to scar any animal or animals resting there. "Thank God" I said.

Nothing was there, my heart was really hoping we could sleep here, but I had to feel out what she thought.

"Want to sleep here?" I pointed and she smiled, `` "sure why not" We were really hungry, and deciding to forget the hunger we but both decided to haul in some more brush to hide us from any night time predators. After we had enough covering I said "So let's hunt". We had been so quiet before this,I spoke out in the silence.

She helped me and we felt like we were going to be safe tonight. I said "you know we were both Girl Scouts "and you said "so" and I answered with the fact that "we should find water and berries maybe?" After about half an hour the only thing we found was more berries. So we gathered as many as we could, stuffing them in our pockets and being careful not to squeeze the juice out. Maybe,we better be careful, so they might not draw animals closer to us" I said.

The next thing we both did was gather piles of dry green soft grass, and some thicker sticks for the bottom for our beds. Heading back to our little cave our minds were only thinking about food, and sleep, and. we were satisfied for tonight. I mentioned the fact that we had no fire for warmth and no light to bring someone to see what we were doing, and it felt safer that way "I'm sure we are safe Elaine". She nodded her weary head. And I saw a tiny smile on her weary face. Every Time I saw her weary I felt so bad, because what if this was all my fault?

Laying there, I tried to go back and remember what the next challenge was for me, and where exactly I was when I saw the ship at sea the first time.

Reminding myself there was bad and good on that ship, I would feel we were going to be luckier this time, but it was my first step to get home.

Laying there in the mouth of the cave, I already could hear Elaine's soft breathing so I knew she was asleep. That was a good thing. Because I absolutely knew there were potentially very bad things that could happen before we figured out how to get home again. but I never would give up never!

As I laid here I could feel a soft breeze blowing the chilled air outside but not inside here. I prayed again for help to take us on this next step, and I felt calm and felt sleep take over my mind.

The early morning damp air sent a chill through me as I stretched and leaned over to see if Elaine was awake too. She was. We were ready today for whatever came.

All I could think of was, it's going to be another long day. Elaine was awake, so I mentioned it was probably time to get going. She yawned and stretched and told me she had actually slept very well. "Of course we did, "I said. "We were both literally worn out, and hungry and we needed some sleep, which I feel like we got last night, for the first time in a long time.

She replied, "I think today is going to be a lucky day". Her smile gave me hope.

I told her I did too. After we shook ourselves out we started forward. Once again believing we were headed somewhere that would point out the way home.

As we walked and absolutely not knowing where we were going, we talked. Both of us were all about a conversation to help pass time. And to keep our heads up with the need to get home she told me a few days ago that we both simply wanted to see anything that could take us both back. After a long day of walking and seeing nothing but more wild countryside, we were very depressed by the time we found another hide away for the night.

Settling down for the evening with not much conversation we were both quiet. "I wish we could have a little fire,"Elaine spoke up.

"So do I but the chance someone or some animal would not only smell us but find us with the firelight is more than we can change, don't you agree"? "Yes of course, I guess I was just speaking out loud my thoughts.".she said.

"I know and I feel the same way. I just think it's time for us to have some luck, don't you?" I saw her smile. I was not sure I was ready to smile, but this was going to be harder for her than me because I had already been lost and found.

The next morning, after waking up and being so happy the long night was over, we started off again. "I'm so hungry," Elaine said, and as I opened my mouth to agree with her that we had not had any food for probably three days now, but right now there was a smell in the wind that smelled like meat being cooked, we looked at each other and thought Maybe today was going to be better.

In the next five minutes there were eight men who burst in front of us, and we both just stood there staring at these men. They were not exactly frightening because they were not holding guns or spears but they did start to ask questions, after they asked me three times I felt safe enough to say my name.

"How did you get here?"was the simple question I heard, so I had to make myself answer him even though I was really afraid but I tried to keep my composure and said "we are lost" staring at them. I saw that not one man had anything else to ask us at that moment. "We are hungry", we both said in unison.

I saw the men looking back and forth at each other.

I stepped up in front of my sister and told them we had gone hiking but we had gotten lost,.then I saw the bewildered look in one man's eyes. And I kept talking, "this is my sister and we were hunting for some meat for our food tonight, but we got lost and somehow I can not remember the way back to where we were camping."then the first man said "camping"? So I spoke up first, yes and we are so hungry" I was hoping to send them off to leave us to search for somewhere, but where was somewhere?

We were both just exhausted so when the smaller guy said where do you live? we just looked at each other and said "nowhere really".

"Where do you come from?" I asked. The man who we thought was in charge said we come from a small town about ten kilometers from here"

Both of us just looked at each other because ten kilometers was less than four miles. And then I asked them what was the name of the hometown"? Both of them looked at us and I felt like something was very wrong here, then he asked us where exactly we lived. Looking at each other Elaine said in a low voice "look at the gun he is holding, because I have seen a gun like that before.".

It was my gut feeling that it looked like a gun we had seen before and it did not look old. So I had to ask "sir exactly where do you come from"? The first man stepped up closer and said "we are from Ayr!"

"Ayr Scotland?" I asked. They both shook their heads yes. So I spoke up again,

"Please tell me what year it is because we have been lost for so long and our minds are not too clear anymore". A tear slipped down his cheek.

And then he said "yes that's right. And the year is 2020."

And then we both looked at the men and fell down on our knees crying. A sudden happiness swelled in my heart, and I grabbed Elaine for suddenly I felt a happiness fill my heart. In a flash they came running to us. Trying to help us get up. After they tried to comfort us we all sat down and tried to undo this strange meeting.

I told Elaine we could not be sure so do not tell everything yet. She nodded.she knew I meant the gold that had to be our ace in the hole.

Before they could give us the once over with more questions I said "how far is the closest town from here?" But the man who looked like the leader stood up and said "where did you think you were?"

We looked at each other and I said "London?"

They just looked bewildered, but then he asked, where did you girls come from and giving them both a once over he saw bodies that were shriveling away, and why do you look like you're starving?

Is there something wrong, have you been harmed, please tell us if someone has hurt you two, because you both look like you've been starved," glancing at his friends waiting for an answer from one of us.

Both of us were trying to think of an answer that would not need to lead to many many questions, so Elaine said out of the blue, before I knew she was going to speak, and tell what had happened,

We were kidnapped some time ago and we have been lost for a long time.

We saw the men share looks like we had to be wrong. So I said ``please Sir can you take us to the nearest town and let us call our relatives to come get us"? They just looked at us.

Then all of a sudden the man who had been asking all the questions said, "yes we will get you to safety."

Then things started to look like we were going to be alright. Within ten minutes they had given us water and a dried biscuit to nibble on.

They were all huddled up talking and hands were going left and right. Elaine asked them if we could get our belongings and when did they want to leave"?

"We are ready" standing up together, both of us carried the gold in separate little bundles, causing no questions.One man asked if we needed help carrying the bags, and we shook our heads no and started walking like the bags were light weight.

It was late in the afternoon when we came up over a hill to see a town below us. We both had been waiting for more questions but they did not ask us anything more. We were quiet and stayed with them step for step. Both of us were sweating but the little town was getting very close by now and we were very quiet, not talking to them and they were not talking to each other at all, just walking.

Then we were in the town. The man we thought was in charge came to us and handed us some pounds, and pointed to a small hotel at the end of the street.

We took his money and thanked him again and again.

We turned and walked away, never looking back. Walked into the small hotel and booked a room. Paying for it and getting the key, we turned to walk down the hall to our room.

When we unlocked the door we dropped the gold and fell across the twin beds. Neither one of us said a single word.

We fell instantly asleep. When we woke up there was someone knocking on our door. "Hello I said" the lady said "do you need anything, we are all going home for the day" we said "no."

As we heard them going away we both jumped up and grabbed the gold.

We just sat there listening to the silence. Then Elaine asked how we got here and we spent the morning asking each other why this and how did that happen. With no real answers.

"The only thing I can say is when we went back to the Antique Store we stepped back in time like I must have before, then she started crying. "This was all my fault, making you go back one more time to where the nightmares started, and I'm so sorry. I also think when we went into that cave to sleep and hide ourselves something happened to take us back home. What do you think?"

I had already thought the cave had something to do with it so thanks to God we are home. Because when we went to sleep that night and woke up we paid little attention to our location. Just happy to be alive and awake I guess. "But we were in London, and now we are in Scotland."Elaine said,

With no money I said,"Elaine said we could take one tiny gold nugget into a store and try to sell it for some money to get a plane ticket back to London". But she said we need to make up our story about how we found or got the piece of gold.

So we spent the afternoon completing our story about the gold. Then we took long baths and ordered food to our room.

Sleep was never far away from either of us, so we went to bed before it got dark.

Sleeping warm and comfortable, we both were so happy when we woke up. wait."

I said ``Please tell me, How did we end up here?"

"I have a plan for changing the gold into pounds. We need money and we have no credit cards and no drivers license but I think my plan will also help us get a plane ticket without our passports."

She was shaking her head, like ok. and I knew she was really worried about the passport thing, so I said here is what we have to do this morning first thing.

We needed to go to the American consulate and report that we were kidnapped. We were held captive on a boat somewhere, and we had no idea where we were until one day the man on the ship got up sick, and we jumped off and ran for our lives.

We can get help from the police here in London,

I actually dreamed about how to change some of the small pieces of gold.

I really think a pawn shop is where we need to go first thing this morning.

"So let's sit down with our tea and decide the story so we both know what to say and when. We can say things that were true but never tell them the date. That is when they would have us committed.

And after we get our story straight, we have to make sure the pawn shop owner doesn't know we have more gold than the tiny piece.

"I think we should maybe tell him we were hiking in the beautiful Scottish countryside, and one day when we were fishing I saw "Then say, we were not too sure it was not just another rock, but when we traveled to London and got our hotel, we took it to a shop in Middlesex and had it tested and it proved to be gold. Then we say we fished and camped for two more weeks, always on the lookout for another sparkly piece of gold. But we never saw another one. It was then we decided to go home.

We had some tea and toast and then we stretched out on the comfortable beds and fell asleep again.

We rested for a couple hours.

Waking up I saw Elaine sitting there on her bed, as if she was waiting for me to wake up. Stretching my arms I said, thinking back over what we've been through I really feel good now, how are you feeling?" "this is how I feel, I am ready to go get some food and a couple tickets to London. And trust me we will not ever go back to those Antique shops that sent us on an adventure we most certainly never want to do again." "Actually, that was not an adventure" We were both laughing when we closed our door and took the elevator to the main floor.

Outside the sun was shining which was a good sign because I was in such a good mood and the rains of London would have made me miserable, first stopping in a tea room we ate our breakfast and had some more tea, after we paid the bill we headed down the street to a solicitors office I had been told by the desk clerk was close and very reputable. Walking in I could tell it was very upscale. The little door bells chimed and a man immediately called out "A jolly good "morn"to you both, and what can I be doing for you this lovely Morn?" He had actually sounded very Irish.

I asked if he could weigh my piece of gold, of course I then told him we had been gold panning in a stream in Scotland, to throw him off if he had a million questions his smile was infectious, and as he motioned to the tiny chairs we both sat down.

He asked "what are you planning today girls"? We just smiled and Elaine spoke and said "hoping to go shopping with the pounds we get from you this morning."

He was very quick to affirm the piece was indeed gold. And he also said it was a very nice piece, and asked if that was all we had. "We have another friend who also found gold with us but we were at different places in the stream."I smiled to myself at her quick words, and I knew she was trying to protect us if he thought we were lying to him, and because I always have this trusting nature that has landed me in trouble many times I let her have the floor and she kept the conversation going as he studied the small piece. It was about half the size of a dime, and we of course had not even a tiny idea of its worth in pounds, so I said "ok sir and how much shopping will we be able to do today with our find"?

He took about ten more minutes and he said he would buy it for 2200 pounds. And his eyes were shining brightly like he just found his pot of gold. So we looked at each other with Elaine giving me the floor to make this decision. The man was anxious so I thought it must be worth more than that so I said "well thanks for the offer Sir but we would not be able to decide until we try a few other places". He jumped at my decision not to sell it and said "maybe I could give a little more, so just what did you want for it"? We looked at each other and I saw Elaine wringing her hands, so I used the situation to my advantage and said "you see my sister said she would not give up her piece, but I talked her into trying to find out just how much we could get for mine", and I looked at her for a reaction and turning back around getting the mans attention I said as I reached out my hand to get it back, "but thanks so much for the price andI think we might just keep it for a souvenir."It was then I saw his face and jowls shiver. And he immediately pulled back his hand and checked it over so I knew a new price was coming. I turned toward Elaine whose eyes were bright and I knew she wanted to press this father also. He took his sweet blessed time doing a check over it again, then he weighed it two times on two different scales. And so now I knew it was worth a lot more than that, so I said as I reached out my hand "thanks so very much but I 'll just hold on to it for a while and if we come to a decision we will immediately come back here to you."

He had already come to another decision, "ok girls I'll be able to give you more because I have a man who was looking for a special gift for a wedding surprise to his future wife and I think this might be it."he was looking and now I saw sweat on his forehead.

"So what is the top dollar you will pay and I have to clear it with Elaine because it is hers". And then I knew if I made him think we had more he would buy this with hopes to buy the other one he thought we had, I turned to my sister and said ``let's sell yours and we still have my piece?"

Her face tightened because we were not planning to tell anyone we had more gold. So I said "mine is smaller but we could do some great shopping with this money, and maybe stay in London longer?"

The man cleared his throat and he asked me if he could see my piece. So I said "it is in the bank vault for safekeeping. I have already called my husband to pick it up. We do know how valuable this is `` as I pointed to the gold in his hands."So give us your top dollar and I mean top dollar because we are not hungry or poor and we do not need your poor offer for our beautiful gold piece."

Elaine was shivering now, from fright that he might try to kill us and steal our gold nugget, but she immediately figured out if I tempted him with more that he would up his price.

So he began to use the calculator as if to resend another offer. Waiting patiently he weighed it one more time then he turned around and said "would

You take" and I stopped him and said "sir make it good or we will have to go. But we might be able to come back in the morning with my piece of gold,if you make it worth our time". Clearing his throat again' which was annoying, he said ``does5000 pounds sound good enough to you"?

Again I looked to Elaine and I said turning around to the man,"give me a minute please". "I am going to ask for 8000 pounds, and in cash is important to us and not a dime less, if you say do it,"I was waiting.

Then she shook her head yes, so I turned around and by impulse cleared my throat and said "here is what we want, and since we both know you knew how much it was worth in the beginning, and so did we, but you tried to simply cheat us out of our gold nugget, we will take 10,000 pounds. And I might even bring mine to you for a price, but trust me mine is bigger" with that said his eyes were bulging out of his head. Sweat was running down his cheeks. And he shook his head yes, after discovering we were not two idiots, but knew exactly what we were doing.

As we started to leave he said "where do you girls stay in London, or what hotel are you using, just in case I want to get in touch with you"?

We waved and just kept walking slamming, his glass door as we left. We knew we needed to get away now. We both had a leary feeling about this strange man, one thing was the large amount of cash in his possession

As we left we were very careful, and figured that was enough money and it would get us home again, but we were feeling danger all around us now and it gave us much to think about, not forgetting we had a huge bag with enough gold nuggets to last a lifetime back at home from the last time I disappeared and brought some gold and diamonds back.

We shook hands and he gave me ten thousand pounds in cash, as I would not accept a check.

As we were leaving, we went down the street to the first hotel we came to,and went in and Elaine went to the front desk and paid for a room for a night, then we went walking, down another couples streets, all the while feeling like we were being followed, to another hotel and did the same thing, except we went out a side door this time. All the time watching to see if someone might be following us.

The next hotel we picked out because it had a front door and two side doors on two different streets.

We went in and acted like we were calling our friend and talked for a minute. And we booked in there too, now we had an edge on making sure we were safe from this man and his friends if he had any, because he did not look like he had a friend anywhere and, he was very tight lipped, with words and conversation and his pounds, and selfish with his attention to us And he almost had a dangerous look about him, which I picked up on the minute we walked into his store.

Heading down another street we watched carefully to make sure we were not being followed. Slipping into a cafe and taking a seat far in the back where we could see who came and left we ate a bite, "we have to keep an eye out for our money changer, I think he was a little too eager, don't you?"

Elaine agreed, and we grabbed sandwiches and went back to the second hotel we checked out.we went to the front desk and asked for a room, adding a quick message with the front desk lady, "we have been followed all day by two creepy guys, please do not tell anyone that you have two American ladies here, we are both scared to death, but both our husbands will be here within the hour, so we do need another room, that are connecting please,.

The same man has been following us all day, "she said "we will not tell anyone anything, be assured, the man that handed out the key replied. "We run a very respectable hotel, Mam.". Then we registered and went up to the room.

Always looking behind us and around the corner, trying to be as safe as we could.

We waited until 9:30 and went out the back door, found a taxi right there and jumped in. When we got to our hotel we rushed up to our room. There was no sign anyone was watching for us.

We had a restless night for sure, waking with every sound in the halls. When the sun finally came up we packed up and it occurred to us that the gold was going to be too heavy, and people at the airport might ask us what is in the bags.

Back in the cave the first night we had sorted out the big rocks and were carrying all the small ones. We put the heavier ones in the suitcase and wrapped them in our clothes. But still it was too heavy. So we sorted them again. Thinking that now we might be able to travel home with the gold in our purses.

We had enough clothes to wrap them up and it would work well unless we were checked at customs.

Sitting there in our room we were thinking of a way to take this home. And Elaine said "I've got an idea, and this might work. We can call for security and take more than half of the pieces to a big bank and take pieces of the gold we could carry.

When we put many pieces in our bi bags and made it possible that we could carry it, we called Hertz for an in town ride and reserved the car and driver for five hours".

When the car and driver arrived, and we had looked through the local phone books and had the addresses we needed for the day, we asked to be taken to a few banks. Not one question was asked. So off we went. My purse was over my shoulder and I stood up as straight as I could as we got in our car, and told the driver where we were needing to go.

At the first bank we sat down and asked about opening a special account with Gold Nuggets. We explained that we worked in Mines and Minerals in the States and we were doing speciality work with some gold claims.

Immediately we had their attention, and were taken into a secure place with guards for protection. We thanked them but assured them we did not have millions of dollars, and asked to use some of our gold as a way to open new accounts. They were very eager to help us. Soon a man came in and opened up his case and I saw all kinds of objects used to weigh and measure our find. The first day we only had a small amount of gold with us. It was very easy for them to weigh our pieces and give us a dollar amount. We were shocked because the first offer was one hundred ninety thousand US dollars for my portion. Then they said they could give us money grams and that we had to pay tax up front. Which we agreed to immediately.

Then it was Elaine's turn, and she turned her bag inside out and we realized she had more than I did.

Her amount was two hundred eighty seven dollars.

We kept the surprise out of our faces and told stories about the many years our relatives had spent digging for this gold. Oh the lies we told. It was like we had practiced for months. They were absolutely impressed. As we walked out of that Bank Elaine said, "we might go on to Hollywood and try out for a leading role now that we have turned into millionaires!"

We did not say a word about the tax thing in the bank of London England. It was mentioned that we might want to open an account to deposit into, and we agreed.

We were not afraid someone might attack or follow us, because we knew no one there and no one knew us. And we did not care at all either, and so we pretended we had to think about it, then we agreed to it and the gold was taken into another room and the money Gram was issued.

The manager asked if we wanted a guard back to our hotel, but we both said we were fine and that no we were not worried.

CHAPTER 33

When we were walking out of the bank with almost half a million dollars we were still in shock.

Elaine suggested we just go to the airport and get a plane ticket tonight and go home. I knew that we still had a lot of gold in the safe in our room, but we could try to get it home in a suitcase and our purses, it wasn't possible to pack the remaining gold pieces so we went back to the bank the next morning, and changed it into Pounds and walked out. What a thought!

We were more than rich. I did not know how to take it all in and my brain would not function as a calculator that afternoon.

So I imagined what was coming next in our lives, and when the husbands find out, are they even going to believe us?

Getting home and not having trouble getting out of the country with all that gold was something we hadn't figured out yet.

The man that took our gold for money was alsoa looming threat.

When we left we both had a creepy feeling that he would be around some corner and we were in danger.

We called in some sandwiches and hot tea and talked a bit. Coming up with this idea was the first thing we talked about. The Gold.

Should we leave it behind, or could we go back to another money changer again? The firstmoney changers were hungry and I already had a feeli

This was still all a mystery to us. Decisions had to be made, and soon.

In the afternoon I told Elaine she was in charge and figured out the plan, a perfect plan. "Elaine, I know what to do. And I know how to keep our gold and keep us safe!" I explained now to her,

Later on after lunch we were getting ready to make some decisions.

There is a sure fire safe way, and I don't know why it took so long to think things through but here it is,

We will call home to say we will be staying one more week. This will make them both mad but the plan is to keep us safe and the money safe too!'

This afternoon you and I will both take some gold pieces and leave the hotel at different times, and get cabs to different banks. We will both go in and open up accounts and get safety deposit boxes in your name at my bank,and in my name at your bank, now that we have pounds in cash to show.. We will both be signers on both but, never going to the same bank together after we open them up. Never going to the same bank would throw anyone watching us off...Elaine said we had turned into very good spies!

We will add our husbands names and every day or so, with the privacy of owning safety deposit boxes no one will ever know what we are doing. It will make it safe, until we can get the husbands here.

Andwe will easily be moving around and be safe too. Taking different cabs everywhere we go.

Elaine said out loud "so you learned all these maneuvers where?"I had been holding my breath to see her reaction.

"Did you forget that maybe I read too much, and I traveled all over the world for the past twenty five years"?

I Asked in between laughing myself silly.. She said I was hoping these little lies were maybe not all lies"?

I knew she was thinking about it but it really did sound safe to me. I had also been planning this in my mind for a week. And long after she was asleep I was planning. After I worked out all the kinks that possibly could go wrong, I pounced on her with my move.

"So we will bring gold pieces to the safety deposit boxes"for safekeeping. Firstwe will go to different money changers, and sell a couple tiny pieces every day for three or more days. Moving around the suburbs of London and never going to the same one twice, even if we get lost it will be exciting and we will get to see more of London. And even being lost in London would be fun when we remember how much money we actually have in ten banks and six hotel rooms!!".

Our story, if asked, was that we bought these from a gem store in the far north of Scotland in Thurso, at a place called "John-O-Groats, Scotland.! Together we both discussed the facts and memorized each word, for future use if needed.

"Lunch was so good", Elaine said, smacking her lips from the BBQ sandwiches we had ordered.

Now thatwe had our plan about moving all our gold, neither one of us let the fear that was ever so close to our every moment, enter into our days anymore.

"We discussed many possibilities but in the end the only one that we were happy with was to call home and tell our husbands.

Not to scare them but it was a matter of life and death. And No we are not dying, but if you do not come we might.

Reaffirming we could be in slight trouble, and we could not talk about it, BUT PLEASE COME ASAP!

We knew it would put the pressure on them but it would also get results.

But we realized there was nothing to do yet, just waiting, our phones started to ring. We both had decided to turn them off. This was a dirty way to get them to London but what else could we do?

Telling them about the gold and wanting their ideas would not help us at all. In fact it would only make more problems. We talked and talked but with no ideas sounding prudent to our situation.

"You know if we tell them they are going to be crazy with worry. On the other hand if we do not tell them and something happens to us, we will be leaving them in the dark, but in my mind, I'm thinking the dark might be the only way Elaine", "Ok here is my idea to add to yours, We need to write letters to both husbands and explain the situation that really has no explanation at all. Or a frantic phone call might work best.

We decided to make those calls today as a matter of fact right now might be the best idea.

Elaine said will you please call first, and I'll take your lead. We need to see if this will work."Ok I'm with you.

So finally we had them buying tickets and from their voices we had them worried big time. With my husband being at first mad, then he was hunting his passport I knew mine was a go, now Elaine had to put the pressure on Jim. So in one hour they had both purchased tickets and were heading to the nearest airport and whatever connections they could make on such short notice.

"Now we will start opening up these bank accounts Ok I asked Elaine?"

"Yes, I'm ready. Pulling out the heavy bag of gold we both had twenty different pieces in a bag in our pockets, we were afraid to use our purses.

Taking a taxi I went one way then she went out later and went a different way.The first Bank was excited when the manager took me into his office and I showed him what I had. Within a few seconds he totally understood the secrecy of keeping the gold somewhere safe. And He was happy to have a new customer. I used the address of EIleen's home, in Ayr Scotland and the one in the states. He of course had a million questions, which I answered the best I could, and waited while they called about our given address in the States.

Explaining where I bought the gold. He was really just interested in getting my business, and I knew it.

I opened three different savings accounts, and a lock box, first.

Walking out I was very careful to take a cab a few blocks from the bank I just came out of. My fear of being followed was ever there in my brain.

Heading to my next Bank I was thinking about how Elaine's first stop went. When I got out of the cab I called her cell phone. She reported that she had become very popular in her first bank stop. I had to laugh because I felt like the Queen from the attention I got. And then I thought at the next bank maybe I should open a small bank account then ask for a small safety deposit box. Keeping my profile low key.I opened four accounts in different ways, in my name then in my husband's name then in both our names, then in our son's name. The safety deposit box had to be in my name only because my husband was not here to sign the form. Oh well tomorrow I will get him there, was in my mind. It took almost four and a half hours and a lot of cab fare but I was finally ready to meet up with Elaine to see how she did.

At the appointed time we met up and Elaine had had good luck also. So now she said "let's sit down and put all these papers in order so we both know where we opened the accounts, and tomorrow while we wait for our husbands to arrive we will have time to go to all of yours and mine and add you to the owners list as a signer to mine and me to yours.

I suggested that we both go to a hair salon and have our hair bleached so we would look very different than when we entered those banks today. Elaine agreed and this was the rest of today's plan. Beauty Shop and food. Then meeting our husbands who by now were probably panicking with not enough information from us, only that we were safe and waiting for them to arrive. We told Jim we had rented a Limousine and then told him "no questions But we disengaged the phone. This made it more suspicious. We were in tears by now laughing. Then Elaine said "when they get here they might want to kill us but when we hold up a big gold nugget he will calm down fast I can see him now!"the ride back to the hotel we had decided to be the one we would stay in appeared and we went, to wait.

"Tomorrow we will add our husbands to the signer papers. "I'm starving," I told her and she was also hungry so we went to get some food. While we were eating both husbands called several times and we could tell they were worried.

"Maybe we should head straight to Heathrow to wait for the plane to land,"I suggested."Yes, I'm thinking they are probably a mess by now. But we could not tell them what we were doing because they would be so worried and the chances we took today opening up all those bank accounts had me looking behind my every step.

"But you know they did not know what we were putting in the safety deposit box" she reminded me.

"And that was a good thing". I said. Her smile let me know she was once again her normal self and these two women would be so happy to see the two husbands. That is until we tell them what had been going on all this time.

"Let's not say anything about the first two weeks and where we had been. And what we had been through,"

I saw her smile and we both agreed. "I was always Happy that we had so much time and no one would have been looking for us, and when we left home we both told our husbands the truth. When we asked for six or eight weeks for our Antiquing vacation. "The only thing I know we will be lectured on was why had we not called for so long? We had already discussed this and had a story ready.

At the airport we waited until we saw both husbands depart. After clearing customs we ran to each other. "I'm sorry we had to lie to you to getyou here but let's go eat so we can explain what has happened. And what we have done. I'm not too sure you are going to be happy but here we are. All safe and sound."

The look on my husband's face said a lot."You told me you were ill"?

And looking at Jim's face I saw worry written all over him too. I smiled at Elaine and mentioned a seat in the airport bar. We walked fast because both husbands were not smiling. We both knew trouble was looming but not for long, and it was hard to not laugh in the face of divorce maybe?? Picking up his beer can, my husband looked at me and his face said "OK"I tried to keep my voice down and the laugh far away, and when I told him we had been kidnapped, he almost passed out. I grabbed his arm and said "look I'm here, and we are both ok,stop and let us explain"! "Let us explain I was almost shouting, and Elaine said to calm downso we can tell them what happened."And I did.. Jim was speechless, but they sat still listening to what had happened to us in that Antique Store to the kidnapping, to the men who found us. We left out the time traveling.

"So now listen because we have something very important and also we might be in danger, but we have covered our steps from the first bank to the next and so on."Both men were speechless.

Then we came to the gold, they were trying so hard to understand but the fact that we never let them know any of this was the hard part of it all.

"Ok"JIm said, now is the time to explain all of it to us. "and he did not look too happy either.

"First we have to tell you about the gold". The men looked from one to the other all the time trying to keep quiet but on the other hand they wanted to strangle us both. "There was no way I could tell you anything, ok?"

But here is the best part. We have several big bags of Gold"! Both men just stared.

We did not know what to do, but after taking one tiny pebble into a money changer and finding out it was worth ten thousand pounds we had to move fast, because what if that man spread the word that two young Americans had brought in gold nuggets?

So we first thought the man was following us and we moved several times. We have not seen him in three days now, so we think he is gone.

The first explosion came from my husband. He stood up and pulled his hair like an idiot then sat back down to cool off. I could see his face and it was blood red. I said "look you can both have heart attacks but I don't think you will like the hospitals here, so just shut up and listen to us" Which they did.

"We made a decision that we both thought would be the answer to the rest ofour lives. money!! "immediately my husband stood up and said "what money"? I tried not to laugh but it wouldn't work and I saw his mad eyes bulging out so I said quietly the "Gold we found"!But that just started it.

"Ok just listen and we need to know if we did the right thing or not.ok?"

Jim was red in th e face too.

"alright spit it out "Elaine's husband was too quiet. I was getting worried so my brain said tell them it all as fast as you can, so I started.

"We found a lot of gold in a creek bed and we picked it up and brought it with us to London, then we had it tested and it was absolutely gold. So now we are afraid and went to a money changer, I see your face, we are fine so just stop",I'm trying to tell you. "Today we made some money plans. We both went to five banks and got safety deposit boxes and split up the gold. We already got then thousand pounds from a creepy looking money changer, who we think followed us, so if you think we were careless and crazy I will totally agree with you, but

stop and just listen to me please, he shut up then, because I thought that they were both so mad we would have a hard time explaining if they would just stop with thekiller looks!

And I continued. Elaine went one way to different banks and I went another. We both added your names to the accounts. By now we were safe and we needed you to come get us and tell us what to do next". Should we leave the gold in those banks and come back next year?

My husband wanted to know where we found the gold, so we both told him.

Then they wanted to know if we still had any in our rooms, and we both said yes again. The looks on their faces can not be described except to say they were both furious with us.Not anything like I was hoping for, like maybe happiness? OH NO THEY WERE NOT HAPPY.

So Elaine said "enough of this, we are safe and yes, IT JUST HAPPENED!and being alone we had to do what we had to do". At that explosion the men became quiet.

I WANTED TO SAY THANK YOU E LAINE BUT THERE WERE STILL KILLER LOOKS SHOOTING OUT OF THEIR EYES.

My husband asked if we could go to our rooms and finish this conversation,"Elaine said yes and stood up. We both followed her to a four seater taxi and droveto our room.

Once we were in the room I said

"Please just sit down and calm down."I had no idea when I brought the gold into the room from our safethat they would go nuts again. That was an understatement.

I laid out the gold on the bed. And then both men went nuts again. Not happy or excited to have this gold all to ourselves, or happy we were safe, no.

Only the fear for us that we knew we would see, but I guess in our minds all that money had blown our minds up to reason and we had certainly lived on the dangerous side for a few days.

But furious with what could have happened. AllI had wanted to do was to make them happy about the gold. And make them happy to see us safe. But not going to happen today, that was clear.

So I stood up and said "I'm going to bed. And started to leave the beautiful room I had found, and

I was so happy pushing away all the bad thoughts and could have beens. That was what it took to calm them down.

Now that they were calm I said ``does anybody have an idea what we can do with the gold?"

Everybody just stared at me as if I should know the answer to that question" ok I was thinking I could pack them in the suitcase with other souvenirs, what do you think? "But I think they might show up on the cameras, so I'm not too sure.

That night the four of them had a few ideas,and some conclusions.

The gold nuggets were going to remain in the safety Deposit boxes and they were going to take some in their suitcases on the plane. The idea was a great one, sounding like it would work with no issues.

Tomorrow they were going to shop for some toy rocks for the kids, and then mix them in with the gold they were taking on the plane. They were going to keep the wrappers in her purse so if they beeped the machine when they searched their purse they could show them the wrappers and say that they were toy rocks, hoping they would let them go through without too much problem.

CHAPTER 34

The next morning they went to the airport, checked in with their toys and their gold, and flew home. The plan was to see if they could get the gold through the xray cameras with them in their purses.

And yes they did go through with no beeps at all when they hand checked the purses and saw the toys they pushed it through and went to the next item coming through the scanner.

After they were seated in the first class section they relaxed and looked around and each one of them had different ideas going through their minds. The ladies had been able to deal with things that no one could describe so it was better left alone.

Some days those memories were hard, and other days it was fine, but then, like in the grocery store, or when a friend dropped by, it seemed that they always had something on their minds, but we both could tell when they stuttered at trying to ask us about our trip, they always wanted to ask us questions about rumors, When they thought we had been traveling and heard rumors that we were kidnapped, there were times when remembering a certain time, or a certain fear, brought secret smiles to both our faces.

On the other hand what the men were really worried about this ordeal, was, was it true? How could it be possible? There were days that the two men met in town to have a coffee and talk about the things their wives tried to explain. They thought Elaine and I didn't know their worries. But we both knew our husbands well enough to know their strange or off handed questions, that came up at odd times, were only them trying to come to grips with what we had told them.

I think it was then that I knew we had really taken some dangerous chances. And I took these things into Elaine's and now I had to o get her through this odd time, and Herbert and Jim, were the only other people in the world who really knew what happened to their wives, and accepted what we told to be true.

Had their wives really survived the terrible things they slowly told.?

Each man had his own opinions but the ladies who had survived those terrible times and lived through this strange happening, would forever remember the events of that time and never really ever have any understanding of how they survived or how it happened or why.

Some Days we got together and talked about certain things and we both know it was absolutely crazy, so we do not talk about it to our friends for fear they would have us committed.

These stories would haunt the sisters for the rest of their lives. Somedays thinking they were crazy, other days knowing they were not, and what they had survived, was a story not to tell many people and unfortunately they only had themselves to talk to about it.

Some Days we both knew the husbands got together and talked about the things their wives told them, about what they had survived, and they knew they would forever be thinking how this had happened, and why them, but other days the Gold and Diamonds were real and that alone made it real!

The one steady fact that would remain forever embedded in their minds, with the other millions of questions, I was sure, was all the unanswered questions of their wives times!! Elaine and I both said like this, and it does make good sense.

"TWO SISTERS DAYS IN ANOTHER TIME!"

And the only other thing that came and went for Glenda was the fact that she had killed a person, but that was in self defense! When that came to her mind she still felt like it was probably just a dream after all!